IN TOO DEEP

In Too DEEP

Island Escapes
SERIES

IN TOO DEEP

Island Escapes Series

ERIN BROCKUS

Chapter One

Steph

THE SLEEK, high-speed ferry boat contained a stowaway. A black crab, its shell four inches across, skittered sideways across the deck for several steps before freezing. I smiled at it from the uncovered, rearmost bench. Heavily decorated in tropical décor, the boat motored over the placid blue water. The crab was less than a foot from me, and I was curious about what it would do. It took a few tentative steps closer to my sandal, then halted again.

"What are you doing here, little guy?" The ferryman trotted over and picked up the crab by one leg, deftly avoiding its pincers as he flung it into the warm waters of the Florida Strait. He turned a smile to me, his shaggy brown hair somewhat tamed by a visor. "He didn't pinch you, did he?"

I laughed. "No. I was wondering how close he'd get to me."

The ferryman, who appeared to be in his forties, relaxed. He wore a white T-shirt, with a second, open shirt covered with dancing flamingos over it. "Good. Some people scream bloody murder if one gets close." He held a hand out to me and we shook. "I'm Lance."

"Steph McIntyre."

He swept an arm out, indicating the boat and its covered interior area, which was as spotless as the bench I sat on. "Welcome to my humble craft. She may not look like much, but she's fast! We've got champagne over there if you're interested," he said, pointing to a large white cooler under the canopy.

Laughing, I shook my head. "Well, it *is* past noon. But I think I'll wait until I'm back on solid ground before drinking. I haven't been on a boat in a while."

"First time here?"

My stomach flopped over, and I worked to keep the smile on my face. "No, I grew up on Sandpiper Cay. I moved away years ago but decided to come back for a vacation."

He nodded sagely. "Always the sign of a local—knowing to pronounce it *key* instead of *kay*."

"Are you related to Vince? He ran the ferry the last time I rode it."

"That's my pop. I took over for him a few years ago."

I smiled as I recognized the resemblance now. "It's been a while since I've been on the island."

"Welcome home, then. Hope you have a great visit." After flashing me a sunny smile, Lance moved to the helm to guide the ferry for the remainder of its sixty-minute voyage from Miami.

I sighed, watching the water speed by the side of the boat. The afternoon was warm and sunny, with billowing clouds racing across the sky. Yet my mood dimmed.

Home... but how can it feel like home?

I'd loved growing up on Sandpiper Cay. Who wouldn't? A beautiful island off the coast of Grand Bahama solely dedicated to making dreams come true. Well, as long as the dreams belonged to guests vacationing there.

As a child, I hadn't had much to do with the resorts on the island, instead spending most of my time in Portsmouth, the part of the island reserved for locals. I had many happy memories of my childhood and had always planned to work on the island when I grew up. But it hadn't worked out that way. Eight years ago, at the age of twenty-two, I'd left Sandpiper Cay for good.

Was the old saying true? That you can never go home again?

Guess I'm about to find out...

I closed my eyes as the cooling breeze wafted over my face. I lived in Tampa, so I was no stranger to the warm sun and balmy weather. But there was something different about Sandpiper Cay. The air was more bracing, the sunshine more vivid. And I had ten luxurious days to enjoy it all.

I swung my legs onto the padded bench and sat sideways, watching the island become larger as we neared. Soon, the Coral Queen Hotel rose above the tree line. The white, twelve-story hotel was a fixture on the island. There were other resorts, but the Coral Queen was the largest, as well as the anchor of the resort portion of the island. Its pure white façade was nearly blinding as the ferry passed into a shallow canal toward its dock. *Coral Queen Hotel* was emblazoned near the roofline in turquoise neon, alongside a bejeweled crown. I couldn't help but grin at my destination. Part of what made the hotel ageless was that it fully embraced its theme, retro and funky. Yet somehow it still remained classy.

Many of the people coming to Sandpiper Cay were there to party. But not me. I had two priorities for my getaway—scuba diving and yoga. Diving would be the challenge and yoga the reward. I glanced at the aquamarine water in the canal, trying to ignore the squirming in my abdomen.

My last dive had been a disaster and part of why I had left Sandpiper Cay to begin with. My friend, Jana, couldn't believe I wanted to vacation alone. But solitude sounded like paradise after the workweek I had just completed. A nearly sixty-hour grind had finished my active projects as a team leader at Allied Insurance. I was free to enjoy my vacation with a clear conscience and nothing left unfinished.

After Lance tied the ferry up to the slip, I said goodbye and stepped onto the broad wooden dock. To my left was Portsmouth, but there was nothing for me there now. Instead, I turned right. The wooden boardwalk continued next to an asphalt road, then ended at a narrow, paved lane that led toward the Coral Queen. I turned and strolled down the lane.

The ferry dock was part of the busy tourist area called Buccaneer Marina. The vibe was fun and boisterous—full of shops, restaurants, and bars. Manicured foliage and palm trees stood between the marina and the lane I walked down, screening the busy area from view. A few golf carts whizzed by, the main mode of transportation on the small island.

Pulling my suitcase behind me, I walked through automatic glass doors and into the lobby of the Coral Queen. Fresh and modern, white couches with vibrant throw pillows were placed around the lobby. A giant wooden Coral Queen etching was the focal point behind the check-in desk. I quickly checked in and received my room key, then crossed to the elevators.

Minutes later, I opened the door to my room on the ninth floor. Posh and updated, the large open room had a gray carpeted floor and a narrow, white dobby-striped comforter on the king-sized bed. Accent pillows in various shades of blue were piled on top. A plush Sandpiper shorebird for sale was placed prominently on the bed. I ducked into the bathroom to find modern double sinks and a huge walk-in shower, all tiled in modern white. Not so standard was the giant glass shorebird, one leg cocked under it, hanging on the wall. I flipped a nearby switch, illuminating it in all its vivid glory.

I laughed, already loving the place. *I lived here for twenty-two years, and this is my first time in an actual room of the place.*

I crossed the main room and swept open the sheer drapes to reveal a stunning ocean view. My breath caught as I unlocked the slider and opened the door. Stepping onto the balcony, I rested my hands against the metal railing, warm and smooth under my fingers. The sparkling ocean vista before me captured my attention. My room faced south, and the afternoon sun was to my right and heading toward the horizon.

The hotel pool lay directly below with pulsing sounds of reggae music coming from the attached bar. Palm trees lined the area between the pool and the beach, and nearby was a wooden building with a thatch roof. Sunlight glinted off some sort of water feature in the front.

"Time to explore a little," I murmured, going back inside.

Downstairs, I passed the main restaurant and exited onto the pool deck. As I neared the beach, the thatch-roofed building came into focus, a red-and-white dive flag flying from the roof. The brick path led to two glass doors, a sign reading *Coral Quest* over them.

Another canal, smaller than the one I entered on the ferry, ran behind the dive shop, and vegetation screened it from view. An expansive free-form display pool lined with large rocks lay in front of the building and was open to the canal. A metal grate prevented any fish or other animals from entering or exiting the pool. I opened the glass door and entered an open room filled with scuba equipment. My nose wrinkled at the sharp scent of neoprene permeating the air.

A Hispanic man about my age with neatly cut black hair stood behind the counter. He smiled at me. "Afternoon."

I approached the counter. "Hi. I was hoping you had space on your morning dive trip tomorrow." Despite diving being one of my main goals for the trip, I'd been too nervous to muster the courage to make reservations in advance. Instead, I let fate make the decision for me.

"Absolutely." The man's English was lightly accented.

Okay, fate chose. I'm diving again.

The question was, did that excite or terrify me?

His smile turned flirty. "I'm Diego, a divemaster here. How many divers are in your party?"

He was a good-looking man, but I wasn't interested in a vacation fling. My last relationship had ended over a year ago, but I wasn't a casual hook-up kind of girl. "I'm Steph. And it's just me diving."

Unease rolled through my stomach again, and I forcibly pushed the negative feelings down. Both at the memory of the experience and of the man I'd dived with that day, who had turned that dive into a nightmare.

He was permanently in the past, right where he belonged.

"I took a refresher in a pool last week in Tampa, but I'm pretty nervous about this," I continued. "I haven't dived in years and my last experience wasn't great. Is there any chance I could get a private guide?"

Diego's flirtatiousness disappeared, and his brown eyes filled with concern. "I'm sure we can work something out. We'll get you diving again. Let me check our schedule." He woke his computer and peered at the terminal before brightening. "You're in luck! Our instructor is free tomorrow morning, and I can schedule him to dive with you. He's great—really reassuring. How does that sound?"

Tension drained from my shoulders. "Perfect! I'm sure I'll be fine. I'd just like a little extra instruction to start."

"He had a cancellation—usually he's booked solid, so it sounds like you've got great timing. You need to rent equipment?"

"Yes, all of it."

Diego passed over a clipboard with several printed pages attached. "If you want to fill out the sign-up form and waiver, I'll get you scheduled. The boat leaves from Buccaneer Marina, behind the hotel. If you show up there at eight forty-five, we'll get you fitted with gear."

As I pushed through the doors into the bright sunshine again, I walked with more confidence, proud of myself for taking on something that frightened me. Diving had been one of my favorite activities once, and it was high time to get over the fears and heartbreaks of the past.

I continued exploring the resort. A cement walkway lined with shops enticed me from across the pool and I headed that way. The ocean was an amazing mixture of blue and aquamarine shades, and I smiled, looking forward to the next morning. A private dive with an instructor was more than I had hoped for. I'd expected to be paired with a divemaster, but instructors had much more training.

I strolled past a clothing boutique and a craft store exhibiting pottery and local wares. On the opposite side of the lane was a glass-fronted building with a long line of fuchsias hanging from a covered walkway. I crossed over, attracted by the riot of pink color, then the name stenciled on the window, *Fuchsia Flow*, sparked my interest further.

I entered a cool lobby with a soothing trickling fountain. A zen rock and sand garden gave the room a calming vibe, and more fuchsias hung in the corners. Soft, ambient music emanated from hidden speakers. A middle-aged woman, her dark, curly hair pulled back into a thick ponytail, was placing rolled-up yoga mats into a large barrel, but no one else was present. Seeing me, she looked up with a smile. "Hello there! My next yoga session doesn't start for forty-five minutes, so you're a little early if that's why you're here."

I found it impossible not to return her smile. "No, I just arrived on the island. But I'd love to sign up for a class tomorrow."

The woman stepped behind a counter made of rose-colored glass. "Are you interested in a beginner or experienced class?"

I was highly experienced, but not about to show off. "An all-levels Vinyasa class would be great."

The woman's brown eyes crinkled as her smile deepened. She had a soothing, approachable way about her that immediately put me at ease. "That's our bread and butter! I'm Monica Crandall. I manage the studio and teach the classes. Would morning or afternoon be better?"

I introduced myself. "Probably afternoon, but I'm not

sure when exactly. This class will be my relaxation after diving in the morning. I'm nervous about it and need to plan some winding-down time."

Monica's smile turned encouraging. "Our dive team is fantastic. They'll take good care of you—don't worry."

I tried to return her smile, but it felt forced. "That's what I'm counting on." I met Monica's warm, interested eyes and found myself opening up. Sometimes it was easier to talk to a stranger. "I haven't been scuba diving in eight years. The last time was when my boyfriend at the time took me on a dive that was way more than I could handle. It put me off the sport. And him."

The yoga instructor reached across the counter and patted my hand. "Let the staff know you're a little worried. They'll make sure you love your dives."

"I've already done that," I said with a more natural smile. "I'm hiring the instructor to dive with me."

The yoga instructor beamed. "Well, there you go! He taught me to dive—you'll love him."

"So I've heard. I guess I could sign up for a late-afternoon yoga class. I'm not sure when we'll be back."

Monica waved a hand at me casually, still smiling. "I have classes all day, and you can drop in if that's more convenient—classes are rarely full. The schedule is posted on the front window and on the TV in your room. Just come by when you're ready. You can charge it to your room afterward."

"That's a great idea. Thanks."

As I left the studio, the beach enticed me, and I ran up to my room. After changing into a sporty bikini, I stepped onto the soft white sand and placed my towel on a lounger. As I stared at the turquoise ocean and stretched out on my back, thoughts of that last dive entered my head.

Until that day, I used to love diving. With Quinn out of the picture, maybe I can love it again. I might be back on Sandpiper Cay again, but he's nowhere near here.

A server came by, asking if I wanted anything to drink. Just because I'd never stayed at the Coral Queen before didn't mean I wasn't familiar with it—everyone who lived on the island was. I grinned at the young woman. "Absolutely. I'm officially on vacation, so bring me a Purple Passion. In the coral crown cup, of course."

As I sipped the sweet concoction from its lavender paper straw, I finally relaxed. The frozen drink was delicious—coconut, mango, and lots of alcohol. I held up the large glass in a toast to the ocean, gripping it by the jeweled stem.

To a badly needed vacation. And to putting old demons in the past where they belong.

Chapter Two

Quinn

A SCHOOL of Atlantic spadefish neared the divers. I turned around to check on my group of six as a dozen of the dinner-plate-sized silver fish swooped in. I halted to enjoy the moment, smiling around my regulator as I exhaled a long line of bubbles. No matter how many dives I led, this never got old.

Spadefish were intensely curious creatures, unlike most fish that either ignored divers or avoided them. The school swam closer, silvery fish with narrow bodies and some with black bars. I loved it when a group of them showed up—they seemed to enjoy the interaction. Two swam up to a diver's bright-yellow fins and nibbled on them. The diver swam on, oblivious. Laughing, I got her attention and pointed. When she turned, the pair of fish hurried to her surprised exhalation, frolicking in the expelled bubbles.

Three more swam up to me, and I hovered motionless. One approached mere inches away from my mask, fluttering through my bubbles. Part of my group was a family with two newly certified teens, all enjoying a vacation at Sandpiper Cay. After the fish swam away, I moved closer to the family, making sure the kids were doing okay. I had a soft spot for kids, and generally loved diving with them. Both signaled they had plenty of air left, and I gave them an enthusiastic okay sign back. The situation wasn't unusual—many kids took to diving easily. It was adults who got the jitters.

Turning back around, I led my group back toward the boat. We swam over a floor of rich coral reef in thirty feet of water. The afternoon was cloudless, and sunlight glittered over the living reef, brightly reflecting the vivid colors. I loved showing guests this dive site, with its mixture of hard and soft corals in purple, green, red, and lavender. Brightly colored fish flitted about, some guarding their homes, others trying to invade them.

The shadow of our boat appeared above, and I signaled the divers to ascend to fifteen feet for our safety stop. As we hovered, a sea turtle swam by, a noticeable chunk missing from its shell. I smiled, recognizing Holly, an injured turtle I'd helped rehabilitate and return to the ocean. She meandered slowly by, her irregular shell not affecting her ability to thrive. I signaled the group to surface.

Another successful day of diving completed.

Back aboard *Aqua Dreams*, Captain Sam drove back to Sandpiper Cay while I made sure everyone got out of their bulky scuba gear with no issues.

One of the teenagers, a girl named Olivia, gave me an appreciative, coy smile. "You working again tomorrow, I hope?"

I smiled professionally back, tolerant of her crush, but not encouraging it. "I'm working, but not sure I'll be on the boat. My student canceled, but I don't know what else the shop has planned. If I'm not leading tomorrow, Diego will be."

The light in her eyes dimmed a bit, but I just nodded and started breaking down the equipment, removing the regulator from the tank valve and opening the broad strap that held the buoyancy compensation device to the tank. Recently turned thirty, I couldn't be less interested in teenage girls.

Not too interested in grown women at the moment, either.

Sandpiper Cay was small, especially Portsmouth, where I lived. And fleeting hook-ups with tourists weren't my style. *I've got plenty to occupy my time.* I didn't miss being in a relationship. At least not one like my late marriage, the effects of which had caused my move back home to Sandpiper Cay.

After we returned to Buccaneer Marina, I rinsed the gear in fresh water and stored it in a storage shed on the dock. When I walked down the alley to the back entrance of the dive shop, I glanced at my dive watch and flinched, confirming it was nearly 4:00 p.m.

Get a move on, man!

I entered the cool interior, passing through the office and into the main room where Diego leafed through a scuba magazine, his chin resting in one palm. I grinned. "You're hard at work, I see."

Diego straightened, smiling. "It's been a slow afternoon. I'm about to close up shop."

"Am I scheduled for anything tomorrow? I knew that woman was going to cancel on me as soon as she realized I wasn't going to sleep with her."

The divemaster broke into laughter. "Yeah, must be tough to be in your shoes."

I gave him a long side-eye. Or tried to. At six-foot-two, I topped Diego by several inches. "Your shoes aren't so different, dude. You're not hurting for female companionship."

"I don't have a *no getting together with guests* rule like Quinn Douglas, dashing dive instructor."

I shrugged and shot him another side-eye. Diego was circumspect, and management didn't mind an occasional involvement between guests and staff as long as they were quiet about it. I grabbed my backpack from behind the counter.

Diego gave me a sly grin. "But to answer your question, I did get you some work. Maybe this lady will be more your style. She came in today and wants a private guide for the morning trip tomorrow. She hasn't dived in a long time and is nervous about it. So I assigned you, nice guy that I am."

I was relieved to have a certified student. "Good. Beats the hell out of doing Discover Scuba Diving in the resort pool all morning."

"Sure. You'll just hand that chore off to me."

"Oh, shut up," I said with a laugh. "I do plenty of thankless tasks around here."

"Yeah, I know." Diego pointed to a nearby clipboard with its filled-out intake form. "If you're curious about your diver, her paperwork's right there."

I waved him off as I dug out my key. "No, thanks. I'll find out about her soon enough."

"She's pretty hot, boss. About your age. Long, light-brown hair and hazel eyes. You could do worse."

I laughed again. Diego had made it a personal mission to hook me up with someone since I'd started working there the previous August. "I don't have time for that. I'm not a monk, just busy. I gotta run—see you tomorrow."

I hurried to the employee parking lot, resisting the urge

to check my watch again. Throwing my backpack in the back seat of my golf cart, I turned the key and headed toward Portsmouth. I hit the accelerator on the electric vehicle, and it sped down the single paved road on Sandpiper Cay, past the tourist marina and dock for the ferry.

Portsmouth was clean and in good repair, but there was no doubt it was a working town, not the tourist portion of the island. Half a mile from the Coral Queen, I entered the downtown area and the road changed to compact sand. Neat shops and businesses lined both sides of the street. I headed toward the working marina and homes in that district.

My parents lived in a one-story wooden cottage—the same one I had grown up in. Hopping out of the golf cart, I trotted up the stairs, seeing it was well past four now. My long legs had no trouble taking the short flight two steps at a time. As I opened the door, my nose was met with a heavenly scent coming from the kitchen at the back of the house.

Sniffing like a curious rabbit, I followed the scent. My mother, Brenda, was using a spatula to lift freshly baked chocolate chip cookies off a baking sheet. She placed them on a wire cooling rack as my seven-year-old son, Liam, transferred cool ones into a plastic storage container.

"That smells amazing!" I said, crossing the small room. The kitchen's oak cabinets and black appliances betrayed that it hadn't been remodeled since the 1990s, but it was welcoming and familiar.

Liam looked up, breaking into a smile. He had my pale blue eyes and almost black hair. His features were more delicate than mine, and though I was undeniably biased, I thought Liam was a gorgeous child. "We made cookies, Dad!"

I tousled the boy's hair as I leaned over to kiss my mother's cheek. "Sorry I'm a little late."

Brows rising, she looked at the wall clock. "We didn't even notice! We've been having so much fun baking." She wore an apron over a T-shirt and shorts, and her shoulder-length hair was now more gray than brown.

As I stuffed a warm cookie in my mouth, Liam pointed with his chin at another container that already had a lid affixed. "Those are for us to take home."

"Even better," I mumbled with my mouth full.

Mom shot me a dirty look, making me smile, though I was smart enough to keep my lips together.

"I'll finish up here," Brenda said, her usual smile returning. "You two can go on home now."

I swallowed, making sure not to talk with my mouth full this time. "You sure?"

"Of course. Scoot!"

"Bye, Grandma!" Liam gave her a hug, scooped up our container of cookies, and ran out of the kitchen.

"Wait for me!" I called and shot my mother an apologetic grin.

She waved at me. "I'll see you tomorrow."

"Thanks, Mom. Tomorrow's soccer practice."

"I remember. I'll drop him off and you can pick him up."

When I returned to the golf cart, Liam was already seated in the passenger seat, his backpack next to mine. After backing out of the driveway, I headed toward our house, a mile away and farther from the ocean. "How was school?"

"Good. Mrs. Jensen liked the story I wrote, and we played soccer at recess."

Liam loved soccer. When he had moved to Sandpiper

Cay full-time the previous fall, the lack of a soccer league had been a major disappointment. I quickly organized a league of six- to eight-year-olds, ten kids in all, and recruited a coach. We joined a rec league in Miami, traveling every Saturday on Lance's ferry to play our games, and sometimes a Miami team visited Sandpiper Cay.

The Sharks weren't the best team in the league, but the fall experiment had been such a smashing success we'd added a second, spring season, which was now nearing the end. Giving Liam access to his favorite activity made me feel slightly less guilty about the recent upheaval the boy had been through.

And now that he's settled and doing well, he's going to get shaken up again.

As I turned onto our street, movement scattered the leaves at the side of the road. "Look!" Liam shouted. "An iguana. A big one!"

"Good eye, bud." I didn't look for the lizard, instead watching my son's happy face as he watched the iguana scamper into the brush.

I pulled the cart under the carport and turned off the engine, plugging it in to recharge as I exited. My house wasn't fancy, but it was clean and well cared for, a one-story cottage with the kitchen and great room in the middle. My master suite was on one end, with two bedrooms and a guest bath on the other. Liam patiently waited for me to unlock the door, then dumped his backpack on the modest kitchen table.

"You have homework tonight?" It was unfathomable to me that first graders had homework, but that was the world I lived in now.

"Only some reading."

"Why don't you pull it out and get it done while I make

dinner? Then we can play some catch in the backyard after we eat."

"Cool," Liam said, unzipping his backpack and removing a book with an illustrated spotted dog on the cover. "I like this book a lot. I should be able to finish it soon."

As I crossed to a cabinet and removed ingredients to make spaghetti with red sauce for dinner, I gave silent thanks for what a well-adjusted, happy boy my son had become.

My life might not have gone in the direction I thought it would, but thank God for Liam. He makes it all worth it.

Chapter Three

Steph

THE ELEVATOR DOORS OPENED, and I stepped out, swinging my beach bag over one shoulder. I glanced at the restaurant as I walked by, but my appetite hadn't increased in the past hour. Earlier, I had only picked at my breakfast, my stomach clenched shut. The sense of accomplishment and anticipation I'd felt yesterday had given way to raw nerves this morning.

Leaving the building, I walked along the brick-paved path toward Buccaneer Marina. Neatly manicured, colorful croton plants lined each side, and palm trees arched overhead. The sky was nearly cloudless, and the morning was almost without a breeze. I tried to take solace in that—how different this morning was from that one eight years ago. Despite trying not to think about it, the memories came crashing back.

That day had dawned steel gray and angry, whitecaps already cresting in the shallows. My then-boyfriend had driven us in one of his family's fishing boats and moored it to the dive site's ball floating on the surface. Quinn had been nearly bouncing with excitement at the prospect of the dive, so I tried to ignore the hard, cold ball forming in my gut at the conditions.

We entered the water, then descended down the line hand over hand. I felt the current's power immediately. It was like an invisible force trying to pull me from the rope and sweep me away.

Quinn had chosen a deep dive. The channel we meant to swim through was over a hundred feet below the surface. As I sank into the depths, the current didn't let up, and when I let go of the line, I had to kick hard just to remain stationary. Quinn was much bigger and stronger. He led, kicking with long, sweeping strokes toward the channel but managing the conditions fine.

I was a different story.

Dread and fear increased steadily, my breathing getting harder and faster. Each frantic breath I sucked through the regulator mouthpiece was like breathing through a straw, and my skin was crawling. Quinn pulled ahead. My heart galloped, my pulse throbbing in my ears as I desperately tried to keep up. I grabbed onto a piece of dead coral to rest for a moment, to slow my wild breathing. My hands shook so violently I could barely hold on.

Quinn drew farther away, now dim within the channel I had yet to reach. I had no way to get his attention, and he had never turned to ensure I was behind him.

Whipping my head behind me, the mooring line was visible in the distance.

The line to the surface. And air. Safety.

I turned forward again, and tears leaked from my eyes as the water rushed over my face. Quinn was too far away now. I couldn't catch up, and all I could hear was my heart thundering in my ears. I was all alone, a hundred feet underwater. Hyperventilating.

In too deep, literally.

I can't do this! I need to get out of here!

I let go of the dead coral and the water shoved me backward, an invisible hand pushing against my chest. Turning around, I let it thrust me toward the line, moving faster and faster. As I neared, I reached out a hand to grab it.

I missed.

No, no!

As I flew by the mooring line, I flipped around again, swimming frantically for the rope and breathing in deep, panicked gasps.

The rope was all that stood between me and being swept away, lost in the blue depths. I kicked as hard as I could, my desperation spiraling quickly into panic. As soon as my hand closed tightly on the rough rope, I began pulling myself up the line to the surface a hundred feet above. I breathed in groaning, crying gasps, and water leaked around my regulator into my mouth.

I coughed, then gagged, moving even faster toward the surface.

All alone.

My dive computer beeped steadily, warning that I was ascending too rapidly. But I didn't care. My only thoughts were of the surface above and the life-giving air it contained.

Panic took over and the memory became hazy. I surfaced and inflated my BCD, clinging to the line and mooring ball with both arms wrapped around it to avoid being swept away. I sobbed, taking great gulps of air that never seemed to fill my lungs.

Some minutes later—I didn't know how many—Quinn

surfaced beside me and grabbed the line, wondering what was wrong.

Why I was crying.

He found out in a hurry as I let him have it with both barrels. He felt terrible, not understanding how overwhelmed and panicked I'd felt.

Of course he hadn't—he'd never once checked on me.

All I could think about was how lucky I was not to have been seriously injured. Or worse. Quinn, the man who supposedly loved me, had left me alone and desperate. How could I trust him after that?

I broke up with him that day.

Now, as I stepped onto the dock, I stomped on the memory and pushed it down a black hole, then slammed the lid shut.

That experience is the last thing I should be thinking about. Today is a new day. I've heard from two people that this instructor is exactly what I need. And my refresher went fine. It's time to move on.

Aqua Dreams was tied up at the end of the dock. I couldn't miss it. A reassuringly large boat, it was made of white fiberglass with a blue canvas shade stretched over the front half.

As I climbed aboard, Diego broke apart from the group he was speaking with and smiled. "Good morning! Follow me and I'll show you where you can put your stuff." He led me under the canopy to the bow and a broad shelf behind the row of windows in front of the captain's console. "Put your stuff here, then I'll introduce you to your instructor."

I set my bag down as a diver in floral swim trunks frowned, looking up from his tank. "Hey, Diego. Can you look at this?"

He glanced over at the man. "Sure. Just a sec."

I smiled at him. "Go ahead. If you point my instructor out, I'll go introduce myself."

"Thanks. He's at the stern—that big, hulking guy." Diego laughed and turned to the diver with the tank issue.

The man in question stood with his back to me, talking to a pair of divers. A momentary unease flowed through me at his familiar stance, and for a fraction of a second, I was certain I was staring at Quinn. Then I smirked, studying him more closely. He had similar dark-brown hair, but it was cut shorter. The man's blue, long-sleeved rash guard clung to his torso, and strong, muscular legs anchored him to the deck.

Quinn never had shoulders and arms like that!

Still nervous about diving, I was slightly reassured at the thought of being paired with such a tall, broad male specimen. His square, relaxed posture positively radiated confidence, even from the back. The diver he spoke with turned back to her tank, and a smile lifted the corners of my mouth as I neared. "Hi. I'm diving with you this morning."

Still facing away, the man cocked his head, like he was concentrating on my words. Then, almost in slow motion, he turned around. His pale blue eyes were vivid paired with his dark hair.

Exactly like I remembered.

They registered blank shock.

Trying to deny the obvious, I darted my eyes all over his face, which was mostly the same. But Quinn was all man now—strong jaw with a hint of scruff, broadly muscled, as well as tall and confident. My heart leaped into my mouth, racing like a horse from the starting gate. A cold sweat broke out on my back, pasting my T-shirt to my skin.

I shook my head as my feet rooted to the fiberglass deck. "No..."

Quinn's mouth hung ajar. He flicked his gaze down to my feet, then up again. He blinked rapidly, like his brain was trying to confirm what his eyes were telling him. "*Steph?*"

My entire body flinched at his tentative use of my name. We stared at each other, my face undoubtedly registering the same wide-eyed stupefaction expressed on his.

Then, without another word, I spun around and marched off the boat.

Chapter Four

Quinn

I WATCHED Steph's hunched form stalk off *Aqua Dreams*, like she was trying to be invisible. I was dimly aware several people were staring, but that was the least of my concerns. Blood roared in my ears. Seeing Steph again had hit me like a literal punch to the stomach. Her straight hair was longer now and tied in a ponytail. Her cheekbones were still sharp, her chin tapering to a soft point. Her wide lips were full—I tried not to remember how kissing them had felt. Had *tasted*. Losing her was the greatest regret of my life, and more than anyone else, I understood why she would be nervous to dive.

Because of me.

Except now I was in a position to make up for my mistake.

I hurried toward the side of the boat, grabbed the railing, and jumped onto the dock. I trotted to catch up. "Steph! Wait a minute."

She increased her pace, drawing her shoulders down even more as she stared at her feet. "Leave me alone, Quinn!"

I joined her side, increasing the length of my stride to keep up. "Will you please stop for a second?"

"No."

"It's okay to be afraid to dive. Let me help you."

Shooting me a furious glare, Steph clenched both hands into fists. "*Help me?* You're the reason I'm afraid!"

I bent my head, keeping my voice soft and reassuring as we rushed down the wooden dock. "I know that. I'd do anything to take that day back, Steph. That experience was what made me want to become a dive instructor. I'd never make another mistake like that. I can help you. Please let me try."

She skidded to a halt and faced me, raising both hands to prop them on her hips. Her face was livid, her eyes blistering. "You can help me? Seriously? Did that really come out of your mouth?"

She was talking about more than the long-ago dive now. That had only been the start of our breakup, but I wanted to focus on the issue at hand. "Yes. You used to love diving, and obviously you want to try again. Here at Sandpiper Cay. I'm not the same dumbass kid I was eight years ago, Steph. About diving or... other things. Let's get back on the boat."

The fire left her eyes, replaced by a deep hurt that was a thousand times worse. Her face closed. "No, Quinn. You had your chance, remember? Leave me alone. I'm going back to my room now."

Heart plummeting to the ground, I watched her walk away.

My steps were much slower back to the boat. After I stepped aboard, Diego pulled me aside.

"What happened there? Where did she go?"

I briefly squeezed my eyes shut. "What happened is a very long story. Steph is my ex-girlfriend. Suffice it to say she isn't interested in diving with me."

Sympathy flickered in Diego's eyes. "Yeah, I can see that. What are you going to do now?"

I blew a frustrated sigh as I stared at my assembled scuba kit. And the one next to it that wouldn't get used now. "I'm all ready to dive, so I'll tag along on the boat and dive by myself."

Diego paused, searching my face. "You okay, man? You look a little shell-shocked."

I laughed weakly. "That's a very good description of how I feel. I haven't seen Steph in eight years. I could use some solo dive time. That will give me a chance to figure out what to do next. Thanks, Diego."

"Don't mention it. I'll tell Sam we're ready to shove off."

My mind was in a tumult as I dove. I tried to concentrate on my peaceful environment, the sensation of being completely weightless and immersed inside another world, but nothing could calm my mind or my emotions.

Diego informed me Steph was a guest at the hotel. So she hadn't moved back to Sandpiper Cay, which meant my time was limited. Maybe I couldn't make up for what had happened after we broke up, but I was sure as hell going to do my best to get Steph diving again. That, at least, I could make up for.

After we finished the morning trip and got the boat cleaned up, one lone beach bag lay in the dry-storage area at the bow.

Captain Sam pointed an ebony finger at it. "Looks like we've got somethin' for the lost and found." His deep Bahamian lilt filled the air.

Diego stared at it before turning to me. "That's Steph's. She must have forgotten it this morning."

Resolve steeled my spine, and I grabbed the canvas beach bag. "I'll bring it back to her."

I strode through the lobby of the Coral Queen, clutching Steph's beach bag in one hand. Laci, a petite blonde from South Carolina, was working behind the front desk. No guests were checking in, and I picked up my pace at the opportunity.

I slipped behind the counter and approached her. "Hey, Laci."

Her head snapped up, and she smiled suggestively as she tipped her head sideways to expose more neck. "Hello there, Quinn. What brings you above the water?"

I resisted a sigh, keeping my tone friendly but professional. Even if I were wanting to go out with a woman, spacey, bleached-blonde Laci wasn't my type. "I need to contact a guest. Can you tell me what room Stephanie McIntyre is in?"

Laci's eyes became round, and she dropped the flirtatiousness. "I can't tell you that! You know we can't give out room numbers."

I smiled, holding up Steph's beach bag. "Relax, I'm not a creeper. She left her bag on the boat, and I need to return it to her." After all, that was the truth, even if it wasn't the whole truth.

Laci relaxed. "Okay, then. I thought you were trying to hook up with her, and that's not like you." She twirled a lock of hair around her finger, and her eyes scanned me up and down.

"No, it's not. The room number, Laci?"

That snapped her out of her trance, and she typed on her keyboard. "She's in room 921." Then she frowned. "I'm still not a hundred percent sure I should be doing this. Don't tell anyone, okay?"

"I promise. Mum's the word. Thanks, Laci." Spinning around, I crossed to the elevators. Nerves jangled in my gut as I rose from the ground floor.

Even though I'd been facing away from Steph that morning, I'd known it was her as soon as she spoke. Seeing her had damn near knocked the wind out of me.

Until she'd recognized me, she had been smiling, and the oxygen fled from my lungs at the sight. Steph had always been the most beautiful woman I'd ever seen, and that hadn't changed. Eight years ago, I'd wanted more than anything to win her back.

Instead, I drove her away for good.

The elevator doors opened, and I stepped out, pausing before the door to room 921. *What am I going to say? How can I convince her to dive with me?* I spent a long moment composing my thoughts, then raised my hand to knock.

I needn't have been so concerned about my words. Steph wasn't there. I knocked five times, but there was no answer. She might have been ignoring me, but I didn't think so. Shoulders sagging, I turned away. When my phone buzzed with a text, I lifted it and was relieved the message was from David, the owner of Coral Quest. If I was available, a couple wanted a refresher in the pool ASAP. I answered immediately.

> Quinn: If they can do it now, I'm on
> my way.

I strode back toward the elevator with renewed purpose. With several hours of my afternoon earmarked, I could try Steph's room later. She had to come back sometime.

Chapter Five

Steph

I HARDLY NOTICED my surroundings as I walked in a daze, my head spinning. I didn't have a destination in mind.

Just away from Quinn.

Quinn!

What is he doing here? How could this happen?

He'd been the last person I wanted to keep tabs on, but my mother had told me a few years ago that he and his wife lived in Fort Lauderdale. My parents had been close to Quinn's, even after our breakup.

My feet took me past the ferry dock and toward Portsmouth. Restless and disoriented, I needed to be in movement and Sandpiper Cay wasn't that large. Fifteen minutes later, I stood in front of my childhood home, a modest two-story bungalow. My parents had moved away after I left the island. They'd been itching for a change, and an active retirement community in Boca Raton had lured them away. They'd been happy there ever since.

My eyes drifted to the second story where my old

bedroom window stared back at me, dusty and unseeing. Instantly, a vivid memory from college filled my mind.

It was the summer before our senior year, and Quinn and I were deliriously in love. We spent every free moment together, exploring the island, diving in the turquoise waters, and losing ourselves in each other's arms. One particularly hot evening, after dinner at his parents' house, he walked me home. As we stood on my front porch, reluctant to say goodnight, Quinn brushed his lips over mine.

"I'm not ready for this night to end." As he murmured against my lips, his voice was huskier, deeper.

"Me neither."

He kissed me again, a slow, lingering kiss that sent every nerve alight inside me. Quinn had always been able to do that to me. When we finally broke apart, he smiled mischievously.

"Watch for me in a little while?" he whispered as moonlight glinted in his eyes.

An hour later, I was lying in bed and pretending to read when a soft tapping sound drew my attention. Peeking through the curtains, Quinn was grinning up at me from the lawn. He tossed a pebble, which pinged against the glass, then another. I couldn't help giggling as I unlocked the window and pushed it open. He quickly scaled the trellis next to my window, his movements as graceful and familiar as a cat's, then slipped into my bedroom.

"You're crazy," I said with a quiet laugh as I pulled him into my arms.

"Crazy about you."

His hands roamed my back, pulling me tighter, and he kissed me deeply. I tasted salt and the faint tang of lime from the margaritas we'd shared at his parents' house. The kiss went on and on, deepening until I was breathless, light-headed. When Quinn finally lifted his head, his breathing was as ragged as mine. His pale blue eyes gleamed in the dim light coming from the streetlamp outside.

"You're so beautiful," he murmured, his fingers trailing lightly over my cheekbone.

As he began to undress me, his movements were slow and deliberate, like he was savoring every inch of my skin. First my shirt, then my bra. His gaze lingered on my breasts as he bent his head to take one hard peak into his mouth. I gasped and dug my fingers into his shoulders. He sucked gently, sending a drawing sensation rolling through me. Quinn continued his journey, his hands and lips working in tandem to remove my shorts and panties. He paused to kiss the inside of my thighs, then trailed his tongue up my abdomen, making me arch against him.

Needing him inside me, I reached for his belt buckle. My fingers were clumsy in my haste. He laughed softly and helped me, tossing his clothes on the floor. I explored his body with my hands, loving every line, every curve. We fell onto the bed in a tangle of limbs and urgent need.

Quinn slid inside me in one smooth, sure movement, and a low moan escaped my lips. Mindful of my parents' room not far away, I bit down on his shoulder to keep quiet. His hands roamed my body, his touch knowing exactly what I craved. He thrust slowly, deeply, his rhythm matching what I needed perfectly. Heat pooled between my legs, building steadily. I dug my nails into his back, needing to anchor myself to him within the whirlwind he was creating inside me.

When my climax finally crested, it washed over me in a wave of pure, exquisite pleasure. My body arched off the bed as a choked cry escaped my lips, muffled against Quinn's shoulder. His own release came moments later, as he said my name into my ear. His voice was hoarse with the effort to keep quiet.

Later, as we lay tangled together, his breath was warm against my neck. And I believed with everything in me that Quinn and I were forever.

Even as the memory faded, I couldn't help but touch my lips. As if I could still feel the ghost of his kiss there. As if I could renew that feeling of absolute connection, of being utterly known and cherished. A connection so intense and so real, it had felt like nothing could ever break us apart.

But that was then.

Quinn and I had both majored in business at the University of Miami, him with a focus on marketing and me on small business. After graduation, I took the job in Tampa.

Far away from both Quinn and Sandpiper Cay.

Where I'd remained, working my way up the corporate ladder at Allied Insurance Company. Working in a cubicle jungle wasn't my dream job, but I was good at it and had quickly become one of the top go-to people. I had a hard time saying no to extra assignments, and an attempt at stress-relief and a better work-life balance had led me to yoga. I quickly fell in love with its quiet precision and the way I could completely let go during a session.

Turning away from the old house and its memories, I headed back the way I'd come. My vacation had only begun, and I refused to let the past ruin it. I let my eyes wander as I walked by the local market, which looked little different than when I had lived in Portsmouth. In the parking lot, my heart nearly stopped as I met the eyes of a woman who looked like Quinn's mother, Brenda. In fact, I was sure it was her. Averting my gaze, I quickly crossed the street and continued toward the hotel. I'd gotten along well with his parents, but that was in another life.

If that was Brenda, I sure don't feel like talking to her.

But as hard as I tried, I couldn't get Quinn's face—hell, all of him—out of my mind. There was no denying he had aged well. *Very* well. He'd obviously been pumping some serious iron, and my physical reaction might be partly why I'd wanted to get away from him so quickly. The situation would be easier if the spark were gone. My mind might want nothing to do with him, but my body had different ideas.

It remembered.

Despite the years that had passed, the ache of losing Quinn was still there, a wound I'd just realized still bled. Seeing him again, so unexpectedly, had left me raw and vulnerable. How could I possibly trust him now?

The Quinn I'd glimpsed this morning was a different man. That was clear even at a glance. And despite the undeniable attraction when I'd first glimpsed him, I was older now, wiser. I knew better than to fall for those pale blue eyes. I'd already learned the hard way what heartbreak felt like.

Quinn making a career of scuba diving was news to me. Recalling his statement that our final dive together had spurred him to be an instructor, I smirked.

Sure, rub it in some more.

But was I being too dismissive? He'd said he became an instructor to prevent anything like that from happening again, and he'd been serious as a heart attack when he'd said it.

I pressed my lips into a grim line. *Don't care. I'm not in the mood for forgiveness. I'm here to have fun, dammit! Maybe I can dive with Diego.*

By the time I reached the ninth floor of the hotel and pulled my key card from the back pocket of my shorts, my troubled mind wasn't much more settled. The whole time I'd been walking, I was beset by the feeling I was forgetting something. I tossed the plastic card on the dresser, trying to figure out what it was. I was pacing back and forth at the foot of the bed when it came to me. I'd been in such a rush to leave the dive boat, I'd left my beach bag behind. A low groan escaped as I turned to pace the other way.

I'll get it later. Maybe I can have someone from the front desk deliver it.

I rubbed both temples with my fingers. My emotions were rising again, frustrated anger growing ever closer to tears. Which I hated. Halting at the foot of the bed, I closed my eyes and concentrated on deep breathing. In through the nose, out through the mouth. The eternal circle. Calming myself.

Opening my eyes, the perfect answer to my angst became clear. I rushed to the dresser and withdrew a pair of yoga pants and a fitted tank top. After changing, I slipped into sandals and headed for Fuchsia Flow.

It was barely past 11:00 a.m., and a class had just started. Though it was considered bad form to barge into a studio late, only two other students were present. I grabbed a mat and slipped in behind them, quietly rolling it out and joining the group in sun salutations.

Monica smiled in welcome, then furrowed her brow as she glanced at the clock.

Yeah, I know. I'm a lot earlier than you thought I'd be.

I shrugged back and let the soothing, familiar movements ease my tired, aching heart.

Nearly an hour later, I lay on my back in savasana. More centered and very glad I'd taken the class, I rolled up into a sitting position. The other guests chatted with each other, leaving quickly. I took my time, coiling the mat neatly, then stepped into the lobby where Monica stood behind the counter.

The yoga instructor smiled at me. "I wasn't expecting you this morning. Change in plans?"

I slid my mat into the barrel, using the time to compose an answer. "This morning didn't work out like I thought it would. I didn't dive, so I decided on yoga instead."

Monica's smile faltered. "Everything okay?"

I breathed a long, drawn-out sigh. "Not really. Remember the ex-boyfriend I told you about who was responsible for me not diving the past eight years?"

"Yes..."

"I met up with him again this morning. Quinn."

Monica's mouth hinged open before she snapped it shut. "*Quinn* is the guy you were talking about?"

I laughed weakly. "How's that for a surprise? I certainly was."

Monica came out from the counter, facing me. She wore black leggings and a bright yellow tank top, *Get Lost in Bali* printed on it. "I have an hour for lunch. You want to join me? Sounds like you have quite a story. I'd like to listen if you need an ear to bend."

My first instinct was to refuse, but Monica's eyes were warm and concerned, and I had felt an empathy between us from the start. "Why not? I didn't have much breakfast, so I could definitely eat."

The resort had a separate cafeteria where employees of the hotel, marina, and associated businesses could take their meals separately from guests. I felt a bit like an undercover agent, being able to see this other side of the resort not usually shown to guests. Though I'd grown up on the island, children were discouraged from hanging out in the resort zone.

We picked up our trays, then snaked through the food service area, choosing the items we wanted. I selected chicken street tacos and an iced tea, and we sat at a table for two.

"I had no idea this existed," I said, looking around the room, relieved to see no sign of Quinn.

"The Coral Queen is a good place to work. I've been here for several years, getting Fuchsia Flow going." Monica took a sip of water, then gave me a measured look. "Speaking of yoga, I could tell you're definitely not a beginner."

I nodded. "I've been practicing yoga for years, and my instructor convinced me to start teaching. I finished my instructor classes a couple of months ago, but I haven't taught anything yet. I might investigate teaching a class or two on weekends."

"That's how I started, and now it's become a full-time career." Monica paused, and I could feel the subject change coming. "I take it you didn't dive with Quinn this morning?"

"No. I was too shocked and... devastated. I walked off the boat and left him there."

"How are you feeling about it now that a few hours have passed?"

I took a bite of my taco, gathering my thoughts. "Unsure. The main reason I came here for my vacation was to dive again. I don't want to give that up because I ran into Quinn. Maybe someone else could work with me."

"How did he react to seeing you again? Did he offer to let Diego work with you instead?"

"No, just the opposite. Quinn was insistent on teaching me himself. Said he wanted to make up for our last dive."

"It must not have worked, since you're here."

I sighed, resting my chin on my palm. "Why should I believe him?"

Monica's warm smile appeared again. "I can understand your reluctance. But, as I said yesterday, Quinn certified me to dive. I can attest that he's a very good instructor. I was really nervous, but by the end of the course, I loved every second I spent underwater."

"Sounds like he learned from his mistake. But I can't help thinking he's the last person I should be diving with."

"If you don't mind me asking, how did you feel seeing him again?"

I tried to put it into words. That I'd felt struck by lightning. "I just wanted to get away from him as soon as possible. I won't lie and say I didn't find him attractive. That was part of the problem." I paused, shaking my head. "He was the same, and yet completely different. Quinn has always been good looking, but... wow."

Monica laughed. "Yeah, he's not hard on the eyes. But you might be interested to know he's not a tomcat at all. He mostly keeps to himself."

I didn't know whether that made things better or worse. I pushed my finished plate away. "I'd better let you get back to work. Thanks for lunch. It was good to talk to someone about this."

"Of course. What's tomorrow going to bring?"

"I haven't decided yet. At the moment, my only plan is to go back to my room and take a nap. I'll figure all this out after that."

"You're welcome to drop into the studio anytime."

I stood. "Thanks. I have a feeling I'm going to be taking you up on that offer."

After returning to my room, I took a long, hot shower, then changed into a comfortable sleep outfit. I crawled into bed for a nap and closed my eyes, but that only clarified the vision of Quinn as he'd appeared that morning.

Every tall, broad, glorious inch of him.

Dammit!

Chapter Six

Quinn

MY REFRESHER STUDENTS were a middle-aged married couple who hadn't dived in ten years. They were both awkward, nervous messes at the beginning of the session, but I worked with them patiently and methodically, delighted to have a thorny problem to distract me from the situation with Steph. After two hours of practice in a corner of the hotel pool, both were able to hover slightly above the bottom, breathing calmly. Each could also flood and clear their mask confidently. Scheduled to dive the following day, both now faced the prospect with anticipation, not nervousness.

After cleaning up, I glanced at my watch. I still had half an hour before I needed to pick up Liam at soccer practice. There was time to try Steph's room again. But instead of trying to plan what I was going to say, I'd let the conversation flow naturally. This was my one chance to make amends, to prove she could trust me. The only way to get through to her was honest sincerity. I couldn't force my words or try to come off rehearsed. It was a bit of a gamble, since I'd never been a smooth talker, but this was a risk I was willing to take.

A small part of my mind pondered a question. *Why do you care, Quinn? Steph was years ago. That ship sailed a long time ago...*

As I was about to knock on her door, my closed hand froze inches away from it. That was a fair question. Ever since seeing her that morning, I'd been consumed with making things right. Why was a woman from my past so important?

Because she wasn't just any woman. And because I'd wronged her.

So be a man and own up to it.

I knocked loudly on the door. When there was no answer, I tried again. After waiting for a long moment, I settled into a long, never-ending rapping.

Eventually, the door flew open.

Steph stood there, glaring, with her hair tousled around her head. She wore a skimpy white tank top and flannel shorts. By sheer force of will, I kept my eyes on her face, refusing to let them move downward, though every fiber of my being wanted to.

"I guess naps aren't allowed?" She snapped the question, her voice dripping with irritation. "I was hoping you'd go away, but you haven't gotten any less stubborn with age, have you?"

A couple walked by, craning their heads to look.

Swallowing thickly, I ignored the butterflies taking flight in my stomach. "I'm sorry I woke you. I came by earlier and didn't get an answer either."

"I was out. Believe it or not, Quinn, I'm not here to answer to your beck and call. What do you want?"

I held up her beach bag. "You left this on the boat. I thought you might want it back."

Her shoulders fell and some of the ire left her face.

"Can I come in? Please?"

She hissed a sigh through her clenched teeth. "Why? I have nothing to say to you."

"I know, but I've got something to say to you. That I *need* to say to you. Please." The couple entered a room four doors down, and the man hesitated, eyeing me hard. "And I'd rather not be a spectacle in the hallway, okay?" I held the bag out to her.

With a long, drawn-out sigh, Steph grabbed it and waved an arm, ushering me in. "Fine. You've got two minutes."

As I stepped into the hotel room, she dragged one hand through her hair, smoothing out the tangles. I couldn't help a quick once-over. She was achingly beautiful, even cross and woken from her nap.

I took a long breath and met her steely eyes. "I'm sorry. For everything."

"I already know that. And guess what? Apologies don't change anything."

"You're right. They don't. But changed behavior does, Steph. I'm a hell of a good dive instructor, and that's *because* of the mistakes I made with you. Let me work with you tomorrow morning."

She crossed her arms and regarded me, her face relaxing. Something flickered in her eyes. For the first time, she wore an expression other than shock or anger. She was tempted.

"I'm not a stupid, cocky boy anymore. I won't let anything happen to you. But I'm not going to pressure you into anything, either. I know you, Steph. All you need is a few good dives, and you can overcome that experience. Let me help. I'll be ready on the boat tomorrow—same time as today. Please show up."

Without waiting for her response, I turned and walked out the door.

I PRACTICALLY RAN to my golf cart. I was cutting the time close and got stuck behind a large delivery truck, one of the few gasoline-powered vehicles on the island. Still, I made it to the soccer field with a few minutes to spare. The Sharks' final game was coming up soon, and a team was coming from Miami to play on Sandpiper Cay.

My mother, wearing a floral dress, stood on the sideline. Normally, she took Liam to practice, then left to start dinner for her and my father, Bruce. Dad used to own several fishing boats but now captained a single one. I joined Mom's side, and we watched Liam at the forward position, racing down the field.

"How was work today?" she asked.

A complete freaking disaster. "Pretty run-of-the-mill."

Mom slowly rolled her head to me, eyeing me steadily. "Are you sure about that? You're standing there stiff as a board."

I had a feeling there was more to her continued presence on the field. "I'm surprised you're still here. Didn't think I'd show up to get Liam?" I said the words with a smile, letting her know I was teasing. And trying to change the subject.

She didn't smile back, instead looking down to brush at

a non-existent crumb on her sleeve. "It's a lovely afternoon, so I wanted to enjoy some sunshine."

My suspicion that something was up turned to certainty. After decades on Sandpiper Cay, my mother avoided the afternoon sun. "Is that right?"

She turned and met my eyes. "All right. I'll tell you. This morning, I saw the strangest thing. I came out of Coconut Market, and... I swear I saw Steph McIntyre walking down the street. She met my eyes, then hurried away."

Shit!

I exhaled a deep sigh. "It was her. Steph's on the island for a vacation. Neither of us knew the other was here, and she showed up on the dive boat this morning. She took one look at me and sped off."

Mom's eyes held a mixture of sympathy and hope. She had always loved Steph and had been crushed when we broke up. The same couldn't be said about my mother's relationship with my ex-wife, Melody. "I'm sorry—that must have been really tough. You haven't talked to her?"

"I did. Just now. I asked her to dive tomorrow with me and let me make up for what happened."

Concern wrinkled my mother's brow. "I hope she does... but tread softly, son. It might take more than one dive for that to happen."

I raked a hand through my short hair but cheered when Liam scored a goal. "Believe me, Mom. I know."

After Liam went to sleep, I went to the spare bedroom where I kept my home gym. I was doing shoulder presses when he screamed. Acutely attuned to my son's distress, I dropped the dumbbells and bolted to Liam's room. A Spiderman nightlight provided soft illumination, and Liam sat up in bed, blinking. I slid next to him and gathered him against my chest. He was warm and slightly damp as my arms encircled him. "Nightmare, buddy?"

"Yeah, but I don't really remember," Liam spoke sleepily, and his eyes were slightly blank. "I was being chased by something, then I woke up. I was confused for a minute."

I kissed the top of his head, glad the dream hadn't shaken him too much. "You're safe. I'll always be here to protect you."

Liam turned sideways and burrowed tighter against me. "I know. Thanks, Dad."

Almost immediately, he grew heavy in my arms. Liam had suffered from nightmares when we first moved to Sandpiper Cay, but they had decreased steadily. He'd been uprooted and relocated to a strange area, so it was an understandable response. I did my best to be a solid, reassuring presence for him. "You want me to get the monster spray? Get rid of anything hiding under the bed?"

Liam giggled in my arms, and the sound filled my heart so much it hurt. "I know the monster spray is just air freshener, Dad."

"It works, though, doesn't it? There aren't any monsters. Think of the world we'd live in without air fresheners. There'd be monsters everywhere."

"I don't need the monster spray. Only you." Liam's voice trailed off.

"I'm right here, baby boy."

I stroked Liam's back, listening as his breaths became longer and steadier. Reluctant to get up, I stayed where I was. My thoughts returned to Steph and whether I'd be on my own the following morning.

I had to admit wanting to see her wasn't only a desire to

make amends. Over the years, I'd convinced myself I was over her. But her effect on me after just a few minutes together showed that for the lie it was. I wanted to see that hurt, guarded look disappear. To hear her laugh and see her smile again.

If she gave me a chance, maybe I could make up for more than that disastrous dive.

Chapter Seven

Steph

THE TROPICAL MORNING was a repeat of the previous day's, weather-wise. Once again, I walked along the brick path toward Buccaneer Marina. Ready to dive. And not ready to dive.

I sure hope I don't regret this.

The previous afternoon, after Quinn left my room, some of the air seemed to leave with him. The room was smaller, dimmer. He'd always had a larger-than-life presence. Many things had changed, but not that. He'd presented his case, then left me to make my own decision.

I had sat on my balcony, deliberating. Then gone to dinner alone and ruminated some more. In the end, I decided to dive, based on the fact that Quinn and I were both rational, grown adults. I needed help, and he could provide that. Wanted to provide that. Two separate people had confirmed his skills as a scuba instructor. Diving with him would be a simple business transaction.

Yeah, I'll just keep telling myself that.

As I walked, the palm trees once again stirred in the soft breeze. When I stepped onto the dock and lifted my gaze to *Aqua Dreams*, my eyes immediately searched for Quinn. He was bent over tanks lining the sides of the stern section of the boat. Several people were already on board, chattering excitedly. Quinn straightened and turned toward me. He wore a red, long-sleeved rash guard, emblazoned with the Coral Quest logo on the front and *Staff* stenciled on one arm.

Sunglasses were perched on his head and his pale blue eyes met mine. A slow smile tugged at his lips, broadening steadily. My heart had been beating fast, but now it went through the roof as he watched me. The air warmed ten degrees as a tingle sizzled down my spine.

Nope. Stop it, body! You're not responding to him. No matter how gorgeous he is. Business transaction, remember?

My girl parts weren't getting the message, so I soundly ignored them and crossed the deck to stand before him.

"I'm really glad to see you." Quinn's voice was soft and warm as I looked up at his towering frame.

"It wasn't an easy decision. But I came here to dive again, and it seemed stupid to let our history get in the way of that. We can both act like grown adults, can't we?" I challenged him with a direct stare, girl parts suitably chastened now.

His smile only faltered slightly. "Of course. Why don't you stow your bag and I'll go over the plan for this morning?"

With a firm nod, I headed toward the dry area.

As we motored to the first dive site, Quinn explained we would dive separately from the main group. "The first dive will be just to get you used to being in the water again. We'll only go to thirty feet. If you feel comfortable after that, on the second dive we'll go to fifty or sixty feet. How are you feeling?"

I watched the aquamarine water race past. "Excited. And nervous, but my refresher class went well."

"Neither of these sites has any current, so it should be like diving in a bathtub. Except more colorful." He grinned and I caught myself smiling back, drawn by his easy confidence. Quinn stood and handed me a black wetsuit. "We're almost there. Time to start getting ready."

I had packed a variety of one-piece and two-piece swimsuits. That morning, I'd put on a blue one-piece, not about to venture into bikini-land with him. But Quinn wasn't checking me out that I could see. Though I couldn't resist a peek from the corner of my eye as he stripped his shirt off, then pulled his wetsuit up all the way. I hadn't imagined it yesterday.

He was *ripped*.

His broad, chiseled chest had a smattering of dark hair, and a defined six-pack rose above his blue board shorts.

Quinn and I were first off the boat. We jumped off the stern platform with a gigantic splash, then slowly descended below the surface. The water was incredibly clear and warm, surrounding me in a comforting embrace. Butterflies flitted about my stomach, so I practiced relaxing my muscles, methodically going from head to foot. I exhaled a long breath of bubbles and continued to descend. Finally, I added air to my BCD as I neared the reef until I floated, neutrally buoyant.

Quinn was attentive, descending at my side and trading okay signals with me to confirm I was ready to proceed. Soon after we started finning over the reef, I lost myself in the colorful, busy world around me. Lavender tube sponges rose toward the sun above, and lacy sea fans waved slowly in the barely perceptible surge. Green parrotfish sped by me, stopping to chomp on the hard coral, and colorful sergeant majors flitted all around us.

Quinn pointed out a tiny yellow eel. I moved to his side, excited to see the creature better. It stared back at us from its hole, opening and closing its mouth as it breathed.

When he gestured to ask how much air I had left, I was surprised to find thirty minutes had passed. I was calm and my heart beat in a slow, steady rhythm. Quinn led us through a broad channel with vibrant coral on both sides, stopping to inspect the reef and showing me the fish and other animals he discovered.

As my fluttery nerves settled, I found myself studying and evaluating Quinn. The man leading me this morning was a far cry from the twenty-two-year-old I'd broken up with. He moved through the water with a quiet, practiced ease that instilled confidence and checked on me regularly.

When I fumbled with the inflator on my BCD, he was right there to help, steadying me as he reminded me how to use the equipment. The dive flew by, and I wasn't ready for it to end when we moved to fifteen feet to complete our safety stop, a three minute hover to remove excess nitrogen from our bodies.

On the second dive, I reached sixty feet with no hesitancy and only minimal nervousness. The placid conditions had a lot to do with that, and I was under no delusions that my emotions would be far different in strong currents or rough seas. But today was a big step. I also couldn't deny some of the ease and confidence I was experiencing was because of Quinn. He never touched me unnecessarily, staying completely professional. But he was focused and concerned at all times, positively oozing skill and proficiency.

After the dive ended, I pulled my T-shirt and board shorts over my swimsuit before joining Quinn by our tanks.

He handed me a bottle of water as we sat on the bench. "Great job. You looked like you dive every day."

Pride surged through my chest at the praise and at my accomplishment. "Thanks. I'm glad I came. I had a great morning and feel like I got a huge monkey off my back."

"You'll only get more confident with experience. Are you diving tomorrow?"

I hesitated, not having firm plans. *Why not? I came here to dive again.* "If you've got room for one more on the boat, sure."

Once again, his mouth stretched into a lazy smile that sent a long, hot roll through my core. Nope, my body was most definitely *not* getting the message.

"I'm leading a group tomorrow, but there's always room for one more."

"Okay. I'll come along." My curiosity to know more about him conflicted with my desire to keep my heart firmly in check. Curiosity won. "How long have you been back on Sandpiper Cay?"

"Since last August. It's been a good move. I like working here a lot."

Without being obvious, I dropped my gaze to his left hand. His bare left hand. Before I could second-guess myself, I asked, "Is Melody here too?"

Quinn clasped his hands around one knee and stared at the deck. "No. We've been divorced for a couple of years." He met my eyes. "Where are you living these days?"

At the news he wasn't married any longer, a strange mixture of happiness and alarm tumbled through me. "Tampa. I'm a lead worker at a big insurance company. I help organize and process new client policies."

He raised one side of his mouth in a smile. "I imagine you're good at that. Organization was always one of your strong suits."

"I seem to have developed a reputation as the person who always gets everything done on time. Which only gets me more work. Still, I like being the one everyone turns to." I fiddled with my regulator, not sure why I was opening up to him like this.

"What's on your agenda this afternoon?"

I whipped my head around, glaring at him. *Are you flirting with me?*

Quinn darted his head back, holding up both hands. "Easy! I was just making conversation."

Heat flushed up my cheeks, and I dropped my eyes. "I'm sorry. I'll probably hang out at the pool, maybe go to a yoga class."

Nodding, Quinn stood, as if he was ready to put some distance between us. "Enjoy the rest of your day. I'll see you tomorrow morning." With that, he moved to the other side of the boat and started removing the regulators and BCDs from our tanks.

I sat alone, unexpectedly disappointed he was no longer at my side.

WHEN I RETURNED to my room, I was relieved to find no text messages from work. I might be an organized person, but my best friend and coworker Jana was not. Part of the sixty-hour week I had just finished involved wrapping up the assignment we oversaw together. While I was on vacation, Jana was organizing our new project, and I wasn't sure she was up to laying the groundwork on her own.

Maybe I'm wrong. No news is good news.

Tossing my phone on the bed, I headed to the bathroom to wash off the salt water. After a shower and lunch, I spent several hours poolside. A combination of a paperback and people-watching kept me entertained for a long time, but eventually, I grew restive.

Replacing my white terrycloth cover-up, I adjusted my sunglasses and headed toward the beach. My route took me by Coral Quest, and this time I stopped to inspect the pool in front. It was deeper than I had suspected. Several tropical fish swam lazily, and I even spotted a moray eel out investigating its domain. At one end, rocks were built up into a tumbling waterfall. At the other end, the open, gated exchange with the canal ensured a steady supply of salt water.

My breath caught as a large sea turtle surfaced at the far end of the pool, near the canal. A young boy, his back to me, leaned over the edge and held out a piece of what looked like a purple kitchen sponge. The turtle stretched out its long, scaly neck and gently took it from the boy's hand, chewing lazily.

I laughed as I crossed to join the boy. "That turtle looks pretty tame!"

With a grin, the boy turned his head to me. My smile froze in place, goose bumps breaking out all over my body. The boy had neat, dark hair and pale blue eyes. With his molded cheekbones and striking eyes, he was a beautiful child. As he met my gaze, I swallowed to wet my suddenly parched throat.

He was also the spitting image of Quinn.

I knew exactly who I was staring at, even if I didn't know his name.

Unaware of my stunned reaction to him, the boy

reached into a nearby bucket for another piece of sponge. "This is Buster. The dive staff rescued him years ago. See how his shell is damaged?" He pointed to a large crack in the turtle's shell, which had been repaired with metal braces. "He can't be returned to the wild, so he lives here."

The boy spoke politely and with obvious enthusiasm. I kneeled at his side, trying not to be obvious as I got my first glimpse of Quinn's son. The turtle finished chewing and blinked up at the boy, who held out another piece of sponge. "The dive staff collects broken fragments of sea sponges, which are his favorites to eat. You want to feed him?"

A delighted smile broke over my face as I accepted the burgundy-colored sponge, pleased at the child's generosity. "I'd love to."

I leaned over the pool and held it out. Buster languidly swam over and took the sponge from my hand, eating it in large mouthfuls. I couldn't help laughing as the reptile performed all this methodically and without rushing.

Then I became acutely aware of the boy next to me. "Do you spend a lot of time feeding him?"

"My dad works at the dive shop, and I spend one afternoon a week here. My grandma drops me off after school when she has bridge club. I usually hang out in the classroom and do my homework." He gave me a bright smile that stole my breath away. It was exactly like Quinn's! "But if there's food for Buster, I feed him instead. Homework can wait!"

"I can see why you'd rather do this. I've never fed a turtle before." He was such a sweet boy, and I couldn't help smiling back at him. "I'm Steph, by the way."

"I'm Liam. Nice to meet you." He held out his hand for me to shake.

"Your dad works here? I was on the dive boat this morning. Does he lead dives?" My heart already knew the answer, but I had to have confirmation.

The boy nodded. "He's the dive instructor here. Quinn Douglas."

"I thought so. I dove with him. You look just like him."

Liam gave me another happy, sunny laugh. "Everyone says that."

Buster finished his snack and approached the side of the pool, lifting his head. I fed him another piece of sponge. "Do you know what kind of turtle this is?"

Liam nodded as he fed Buster a green sponge. "Hawksbill. See how the front of his beak comes to a point? Sponges are what hawksbills usually eat, and my dad likes Buster's diet to be as natural as possible."

My eye drifted to the sign next to the waterfall that read *Please don't feed the turtle! Enjoy watching him, but the wrong food can make him sick or worse. Thank you.*

"Sounds like Buster has a nice home."

"My dad says he's living the high life here. Never has to work a day in his life."

"I can see that. I'm jealous!"

We were both laughing when the glass door to the dive shop opened, and Quinn walked out, zipping a dry bag shut. "You ready to head out, buddy?"

He saw Liam and me kneeling side by side and stumbled to a stop, his eyes bulging.

Liam rose and brushed the sand off his knees. "Yeah. Let me get my backpack from inside." He stepped around me and entered the dive shop.

My heart nearly stopped, my attention riveted by Quinn's shocked gaze.

He seemed incapable of speech, standing there staring at me. So I slowly stood, breaking the trance. "Liam was showing me how to feed Buster. He's a wonderful boy, Quinn."

"Yes," he said, his voice thick and gruff. "He is." A tumult of emotions rolled across Quinn's face, replacing shock. Regret, fear, and a tense tightness I'd never seen before.

"Does he live with you?" Joint custody when Quinn lived offshore would be difficult.

He hesitated, his jaw working. "Yes, he goes to school here. Like we did."

I was still reeling at meeting the boy. The knowledge of him was one thing, but actually speaking to him was another. But he was clearly a sweet, polite child with no understanding or culpability for the damage his presence had brought to Quinn and me.

Liam pushed out the door, settling his backpack on his shoulders. Without looking, Quinn wrapped an arm around his shoulders, pulling him close. "I'm done for the day, so let's head home, Liam."

His tight voice made the boy look up at him, his face clouding with confusion. Seeing his father's expression, he shifted his gaze to me, regarding me intently.

Quinn took a long, sharp breath, clearly still shaken. "See you on the boat tomorrow?"

What he was asking was clear. Quinn wanted me there, but he also understood what seeing Liam might do to me. I smiled as I met Liam's eyes.

An innocent boy whose parents weren't together anymore.

I turned to Quinn and nodded. "You will. See you in the morning."

Chapter Eight

Quinn

I RESTED a hand protectively on Liam's backpack as we walked toward the parking lot, my mind racing over what Steph might have said to my son. At least she hadn't appeared angry—a little shocked, yes. But that was understandable, to say the least. And after spending all morning with her, I wanted to see her again.

But my first responsibility was to Liam, and seeing them together brought that home in no uncertain terms.

Since getting divorced two years prior, I had only been in one relationship, an ill-advised dalliance with a coworker in Fort Lauderdale that had ended almost before it began. The woman had never interacted with my son. A fact I had been grateful for when our relationship fizzled.

Liam had adjusted as well as could be expected to my divorce from Melody. *I guess divorce is common enough that he understands we're never getting back together.*

When we separated, I moved to a nearby apartment, and we had shared custody. But when she moved with her boyfriend to Destin the previous summer, I insisted on a new custody arrangement. And now I was here on Sandpiper Cay again, but with Liam this time.

Steph's reappearance had left me a confused, conflicted mess. She was here on vacation, not permanently. And we weren't together in any way. Introducing her to Liam had never even crossed my mind.

And seeing them together had shocked me to the core, causing a wave of protectiveness to rush over me. Because that surge of emotion had been directed toward *both* of them. Toward Liam obviously, but I'd also felt the need to shield Steph from any further pain. She was already dealing with the turmoil of seeing me again. Then she came face-to-face with my son.

With the result of those miserable, torturous few months after that final dive.

I climbed into the driver's seat and pulled out of the parking lot. "Did you have a good time feeding Buster?"

Liam nodded. "He loves sponges. That lady came by and wanted to help. She said she dove with you this morning."

I tightened my grip on the wheel. *What else did she say? What else should I say?* "She's here on vacation. We used to know each other... a long time ago."

Liam nodded, like he'd expected that answer.

"Did you two talk a lot?" I asked, keeping my voice soft even as my heart rate sprinted forward.

"No, mostly about Buster."

Liam dropped the subject, turning to the sleepover planned at his friend Grayson's the following night. Tension drained out of my body, and that relief was partly due to confirmation that Steph hadn't said anything about our history.

She's never been the vindictive type. She wouldn't take out her anger at me on Liam.

But did I know that for certain? I hadn't seen the woman in eight years. Liam had been through enough, and I wasn't going to add to his worries.

As we drove past the ferry dock toward Portsmouth, Liam sighed. "I hope I make friends at Mom's. I'm going to miss Grayson over the summer."

Not as much as I'm going to miss you.

My stomach knotted just thinking about the long stretch of time rapidly approaching. "Of course you will. Plus, I'm sure you'll have plenty to keep you busy while you're there." We had less than two weeks left before Liam left to spend the summer with Melody.

"Mom said she's taking me to an adventure park right away."

"That'll be fun."

Liam gave me a big smile, his equilibrium apparently restored. "It will. Can we have Froot Loops for dinner?"

That change in subject was enough to make me take my eyes off the road to stare at my son. "What? When have we *ever* had Froot Loops?"

Liam giggled, a sound that warmed me to the center of my soul. "A boy in my class had them for dinner. He visited his dad, who couldn't cook, and he didn't have time to go to the store. So they ate cereal."

I repressed a shudder. After moving out, I'd taken a series of cooking classes at a community center in Fort Lauderdale so I would never face that situation. "Hey, you said you liked my cooking."

"I do. I just thought it was funny to eat cereal for dinner."

"Yeah, well, upgrade your standards a little, bud."

Liam laughed again. The breeze blew his hair off his forehead as the golf cart turned a corner. "You got it. How about steak and lobster, then?"

"How about teriyaki chicken and mashed potatoes? And vegetables!"

Liam made a face, but his good nature won out. "All right. Ice cream for dessert?"

"Deal."

When we got home, Liam turned on the TV while I headed for the kitchen. I'd had chicken breasts marinating in teriyaki sauce all day. As I prepared dinner, my mind returned to Steph and the morning we'd spent together. At the start, I'd been a bundle of nerves, wondering if she'd show up to dive. Then, when she stood before me, I thought my smile might actually break my face.

I was still powerfully, viscerally attracted to her. But she wasn't exactly happy to see me, and I was conflicted and confused about seeing her again. Except for wanting to help her dive again. So I'd kept my hands to myself, even more than I would normally. Never flirtatious with students, I would provide a comforting touch when needed. But not that morning with Steph, though I'd checked her out when I knew she couldn't see me. She still had curves in all the right places. Soft, creamy skin. Exactly like I remembered.

As the hours passed, Steph had visibly warmed to me, and I had to admit there was more going on than my desire to make up for being such an asshole on that dive years ago. I wanted more.

I wanted her.

But could interacting for a few days make up for how badly I'd hurt her? Plus, I was nursing my own pain from that time.

And what about Liam?

Chapter Nine

Steph

I LENGTHENED both arms over my head, then leaned back into warrior II pose and held it. The inherent strength and power of the pose surged through me, and I drew from it. I was nearing the end of my second yoga session of the afternoon and the final class scheduled for the day.

After Quinn had left with his arm wrapped tightly around his son's shoulders, my emotions had been tied up in a giant knot I couldn't untangle. Once again, yoga had come to my rescue. Monica wore another Bali tank top, this one with *Bali... The Island of the Gods* printed across it, and she'd smiled at me as I entered the first class. But when I'd stayed for the second, the instructor's gaze had turned more assessing.

This second class was sparsely attended, many guests preferring to get ready for the evening's adventures. *Not much adventure for me tonight.* I was the last one in line to pay the bill and stepped forward to sign the room charge.

"How was your second full day at the Coral Queen?"

Monica asked. "Since you didn't come in until late after-noon, you must have been busy."

"It's been a day of ups and downs." *And shocks.*

"Involving Quinn?"

"Definitely involving Quinn."

Monica gave me a sympathetic smile. "I can't deny being curious about your situation, and I'm a pretty good listener. You want to have a drink?"

I needed a sounding board badly. "That sounds great. Do you have an employee bar, or should we hit the pool bar?"

Monica laughed. "Employee bars might be a bit much, even for Sandpiper Cay. Let's head to the pool."

We both ordered glasses of white wine and I told her about diving for the first time in eight years. "By the end of it, I was *so* much more comfortable. Quinn did a great job picking sites to build my confidence."

"How did you two get along?"

I sipped my wine, gathering my thoughts. "Carefully. He went out of his way to be professional and made sure I was comfortable with what we were doing."

"But no flames rekindling?"

"Well, I'm not blind," I said with a laugh. "Quinn was gorgeous when we dated, and he's only improved over the years. So yeah—the spark is still there. But it's so compli-cated. A lot of hurt feelings, mostly on my end."

"Because of how things ended after that last dive."

Not exactly...

Monica took a breath to speak, then closed her mouth, sipping her drink instead.

I cocked my head. "What were you about to say?"

"It's nothing. We've only known each other for two days. I've got no right to butt into your business."

A smile tugged at my lips. "That's why we're having this drink, Monica. Since you know Quinn, I'm interested in your opinion. You can tell me what's on your mind."

Monica swirled her wine. "It's just that... Quinn did something careless and thoughtless on that dive. *Years* ago." She met my eyes. "Now he's trying to make up for it. Do you think maybe you're being a little hard on him?"

I sighed and stared at the pool with unfocused eyes. "We're going to need a refill for this." Draining the rest of my glass, I signaled our server for another round before meeting Monica's eyes. "I can be judgy, and I have a tendency to hold a grudge when I've been wronged. That's one of the reasons I got into yoga and meditation—to work on that side of myself. Learn to live more in the present."

I smiled at the server as our glasses were refilled. "That dive happened during our senior year in college, while we were home on winter break. I broke it off with Quinn and we went back to school, living separate lives. I stewed in my righteous indignation, and he got involved with someone new. We both went to school with her on Sandpiper Cay, and all three of us attended the University of Miami. I never liked Melody. She was shallow and clingy. She'd been after Quinn for years, and I was jealous seeing them together. But more than that, I came to realize what you pointed out."

I shook my head and leaned my elbows on the table. This was the hard part of the story. "Quinn made a mistake. He tried to talk to me several times about that dive and getting back together. Finally, he gave up and moved on. But I was miserable. I missed him so much, and I finally realized the only thing keeping us apart was *me*. It was time to let go of my anger and act like an adult. We were twenty-two, for God's sake."

"That sounds like a very human reaction. What happened?"

I took a long breath that seemed to do nothing to fill my lungs. "I went to see him almost three months after we broke up, and he'd been with Melody for two months. I finally talked to him. Said I was sorry. That I overreacted to the situation and asked if we could try again. Before he got serious with Melody. I couldn't fathom that he could *want* to be with her."

"And what did he say?" Monica asked, her voice quiet.

"He looked me straight in the eye and told me Melody was pregnant. And they were getting married at the courthouse the following week."

"Oh my God!" Monica flopped back in her chair.

"Yeah. I could actually *feel* my heart break. He looked as devastated as I felt. I started crying and ran away. I never spoke to him again until yesterday. He married Melody, and we graduated. I got a job in Tampa. My parents left Sandpiper Cay, so I had no reason to come back here. I heard Quinn and Melody had a boy and moved to Miami, but I never kept tabs on him. I never would have come here if I'd known he was back."

Monica squeezed my numb hand. "I'm so sorry. That must have been awful. I can see why meeting him again was such a shock."

"I got another shock this afternoon when I met his son, Liam. He's a carbon copy of Quinn."

"I wondered if you knew about Liam. He's kind of a regular around here."

I nodded. "That's what he said. He's a very sweet boy. What happened wasn't anyone's fault. I see that now. And it certainly wasn't Liam's. Quinn didn't cheat on me—the whole situation was just... life happening. In the worst way."

"And now he has his life here and you have yours in Tampa."

I snorted and took a drink, pleasantly buzzed now. "Believe me, mine's nothing to write home about. I like my job, but it sure isn't what I thought I'd be doing." I forced a smile and pointed to Monica's tank top. "Maybe I'll run away to Bali and teach yoga!"

We both laughed and touched glasses before drinking. Monica swallowed, then eyed me steadily. "You know, there might be another option."

"What? I'm all ears."

"I get wanderlust easily—I'm kind of a vagabond. And I've always dreamed of living in Bali, as you can probably tell from my shirts!" Monica laughed and took a sip of wine. Then her expression sobered. "Only senior management knows this, but I accepted a position in Bali at a small resort with a yoga studio. So Fuchsia Flow is going to need an instructor very soon."

My mouth dropped open. "I couldn't do that!"

"Why not? I can tell by watching you that you're a natural. And you have the training."

"I've never even taught a class!"

Monica shrugged. "Everyone starts somewhere. Maybe we can teach a class together or something while you're here. And if you got the job, it would give you and Quinn a chance to reconnect. If that's what you want..."

My heart was winding up to fly out of my chest. "He gave no indication he's interested in me."

"Other than running you down—twice—to get you to dive with him."

"Because he wanted to make amends. Not because he wanted to see *me*."

Monica arched a brow. "You sure about that?"

I paused. No, I wasn't sure about that.

"After the story you told me, I wouldn't be surprised if Quinn wants some signal from you that you're interested. The question is, are you?"

I gazed at the sun as it slowly disappeared into the ocean horizon. It left a crimson swath of sky in its wake. Just picturing Quinn when he'd had his shirt off sent a delicious quiver of desire through me. "Physically—yes. I can't deny that. But emotionally? That's a very big ask."

And if something physical did happen between us in the next few days, could I keep my heart from following?

Chapter Ten

Quinn

THE NEXT MORNING, I slid two scuba tanks into their plastic holders behind the side benches of *Aqua Dreams*. Next, I attached the BCD and regulator, my motions rote and automatic. Which was good because I couldn't concentrate on my job anyway.

Despite my best efforts, my eyes darted to the dock every few seconds, watching for Steph to appear. A restless night hadn't made me any less confused about my feelings for her, or where I wanted things to go between us.

I should be grateful if she isn't hostile toward me. If she shows up at all.

I caught movement out of the corner of my eye, but it wasn't her. Another couple boarded, and the man headed toward me. "We're having a problem with Angela's mask. Can you take a look at it?"

"Sure." I took the mask, quickly discovering the strap needed to be rethreaded. In no time, I had it set to rights and handed it back to the man. Another glance at the wooden dock revealed it was empty, and a hard, tight knot formed in my stomach. It was nearly time to go. Pressing my lips into a tight line, I turned toward the bow.

And there she stood.

My breath stalled in my lungs. Steph must have come on board when I was adjusting the mask. After she placed her bag in the dry area, she turned. Our eyes met.

And held.

The knot in my gut relaxed at her smile. Steph's light-brown hair was braided into a tail down her back. Wearing a tight, long-sleeved rash guard and board shorts, she approached and stared up at me, a sparkle in her eye. "Good morning. This looks like a great day for diving." She held an arm out to indicate the flat water and sunny sky.

I tried to hide my relief, not wanting to appear desperate, and gave her a full smile that hopefully didn't look too stupid. "Doesn't get much better. You'll do great today."

"I'm less nervous than yesterday morning, so that's progress."

I forced my heart to slow. Steph had a smattering of freckles on her cheeks, and I couldn't stop imagining what it would be like to kiss them. "I'm glad you're here."

"Me too, Quinn. I guess we both got a shock yesterday."

Our eyes were still locked together, and both our smiles widened. I broke into laughter. "That's pretty much the understatement of the century."

I had so many questions for her. *What have you been doing for the last eight years? Why are you here alone?*

I didn't know for certain she was on a solo vacation, but I'd put money on it. She'd been by herself every time I'd seen her, and her room was registered only in her name. But a busy dive boat wasn't the place to ask. *If things go well this morning, I'll ask her to help me with Buster. She obviously enjoyed interacting with him.*

With a solid plan at last, I went to work.

I talked to Sam and Diego earlier and we chose two fun, easy sites that would be perfect for Steph. Of course, I hadn't said outright that was why I wanted to go there, but Diego had given me a sly smile. He knew something was going on between Steph and me, though he hadn't pried. Diego was a good friend. I would confide in him if and when it was time.

Turtle Town was a patch reef, with sandy lanes spaced between hillocks of coral covered with fans, sponges, and soft coral. Turtles loved this kind of terrain. During the dive, I spotted three, the final one a rare loggerhead resting in the sand. I crept closer, my group fanning out beside me. The turtle turned its massive, namesake head toward me and stared benignly as it rubbed its shell on a piece of coral.

Steph appeared at my side. There was a gentle surge that morning, and it pushed her into me. With a squeak, she grabbed onto my arm for support, using me to steady herself as she inspected the large turtle. I froze, afraid to move and disturb the fact that Steph had reached for me of her own free will. The turtle pushed off the sand, using its powerful flippers to rise toward the surface and air. Steph watched it go, then turned to me. Her eyes gleamed behind her mask, her happiness at the encounter shining through. I couldn't look away. Seeing her again had scratched an itch I didn't know I'd had. This was about more than making up for poor choices years ago.

I wanted another shot with her.

After we reboarded, I kept stealing glances at her. The previous morning, she'd worn a one-piece swimsuit. But today, a dark-red sport bikini hugged her hourglass figure and covered her perfect, full breasts—a vivid reminder of what I'd lost.

As the morning wore on, I caught her staring straight at me several times, further cementing my certainty our connection was still there. But every time I thought about asking her out, my hands grew clammy, like I was some nervous teenager. I kept dithering, and before I knew it, we were back at the marina. As she gathered her things, my heart leaped into my throat.

"Steph?"

Her greenish-hazel eyes met mine, inquisitive.

Summoning my courage, I approached her side and spoke quietly. "Listen, I'm cleaning Buster's shell this afternoon."

Her brows furrowed. "Oh? Is something wrong with him?"

"Nah—just part of the usual routine. It's a pretty involved process, and I was wondering if you might want to help."

Confusion clouded her features. "Help? Why?"

Heat flashed across my face, and I hoped I didn't sound too obvious. "It's always easier with two people. And..." I hesitated, meeting her gaze. "I thought it might be nice to spend some time together. Away from all the chaos of the dive boat."

A flicker of something—curiosity, maybe even interest—crossed her face. "Okay," she said slowly. "That sounds kind of fun. I'll help."

Relief washed over me, tinged with something that felt suspiciously like elation. "Great. I'll meet you by the pool around four?"

"Sounds good. See you then."

With a smile, Steph gathered her things and walked off

the boat. My heart felt lighter, like it might just fly out of my chest. We'd just made a small step. But right now, it felt like a huge leap out of the past.

At 4:00 P.M., I was pacing the back room of Coral Quest. My stomach churned with nervous energy. I checked the bucket of cleaning supplies for the third time, making sure I had everything. Sponges, scrub brushes, antibacterial wash —all present and accounted for.

Get a grip, Douglas. It's just cleaning a turtle's shell. You've done it a hundred times.

Except this time, everything was different. And no amount of double checking would change that. I glanced at my watch. Five minutes late. Maybe she'd changed her mind. Maybe she'd realized spending a couple of hours with me scrubbing algae wasn't exactly her idea of a good time.

Disappointment stabbed through me.

The walls closed in me, and I had to get outside again. Squaring my shoulders, I returned to the pool. Sam, a moray eel we'd rescued and who now lived there permanently, was out and winding around the rocks lining the bottom, looking for crabs I liked to hide for him. Buster was resting under the waterfall, one of his favorite places.

Unable to help myself, I looked down the walkway. Relief, so profound it made my knees weak, flooded through me. Steph strode toward me, her movements lithe and athletic. She'd changed into a pair of jean shorts and a sleeveless turquoise top. While not low cut, the shirt did nothing to hide her spectacular breasts. Her hair was tied back in a turtle-cleaning-appropriate ponytail. I couldn't tear my eyes away. She was even more beautiful than I remembered—hell, I was pretty sure she *was* more beautiful now. And seeing her again, after thinking I'd lost her for good, sent a powerful wave of longing through me.

"Hey," she said, her smile hesitant. "I got held up at the elevator. Am I too late?"

"No, not at all." My voice came out rougher than I intended. I cleared my throat, suddenly self-conscious under her warm gaze. "Ready to get started?"

Chapter Eleven

Quinn

"SURE." Steph nodded, and a tentative smile raised her lips. "I have to admit, this will be a new experience for me."

Her smile made my gut unclench some more. "Well, that's what travel is about, right?"

"Exactly." She shaded her eyes and pointed to the waterfall. "He looks pretty content. Does he come when you call his name?" She shot me a teasing smile that damn near collapsed my lungs.

"No, but he can be bribed." I sat down on the edge of the pool and grabbed a piece of sponge from a nearby bucket. I waved it in the water, hoping Sam would stay well away. The eel wouldn't be tempted by the sponge, but the movement might draw him. I spoke without taking my eyes from the scene. "Turtles have an acute sense of smell. I imagine this will bring him over."

Sure enough, Buster's eyes slowly opened, and he trundled off his rocky perch. I darted my eyes to Steph and was rewarded when she broke into a dazzling smile as he lazily swam over and took the sponge fragment from my hand.

"He's a lot bigger than the hawksbill we saw diving," Steph said, watching Buster devour the sponge.

"Yeah, he's a healthy guy. Full-grown hawksbills can get up to 150 pounds." I tossed another piece of sponge into the water, and Buster snapped it up. "Ready to give him a spa day?"

Steph's eyes widened. "Do we just pick him up?"

I grinned. "Pretty much. It's easier than you'd think. Want to help?"

She nodded eagerly, and together we moved to opposite sides of the turtle. I grasped him firmly under his shell, just behind his front flippers, while Steph got a good hold in front of his rear ones.

I winked at her, unable to resist. "Okay, on three. One, two, three!"

We lifted Buster out of the water, his powerful legs kicking for a moment before he settled. He was heavier than he looked, but I hefted him easily, surprised at the surge of masculine pride that ran through me when Steph's eyes widened in appreciation.

"Now I see where you got those muscles!"

My smile widened, and I tried to keep my shrug nonchalant as we scrabbled away from the pool. "Years of lugging scuba tanks around."

We carried Buster down the short walkway to a blue kiddie pool I'd set up behind the dive shop. I lowered him carefully into the water, which was only a couple of inches deep. He settled and blinked lazily.

"He seems pretty relaxed about all this," Steph said. She crouched at the edge of the pool, her fingers brushing lightly over Buster's shell.

"He's used to it. We clean his shell every few weeks. Ready?"

"Let's do it."

I dipped my scrub brush into the bucket of soapy water and gently rubbed at a patch of algae near the edge of Buster's shell. He stretched out his neck, and his eyes took on a slightly glazed look.

Steph burst into laughter. "Looks like he's loving it."

"Turtles have nerve endings in their shells," I explained. "So it probably feels like a good back scratch to him."

Still smiling, she grabbed a brush and dipped it in the bucket. "You learn something new every day." Moving to the other side of the pool, she started scrubbing the shell near Buster's tail.

I watched her for a moment, my heart squeezing at how natural—how right—it felt to be working alongside her. As she scrubbed, her biceps and triceps worked under her smooth skin.

"You're working like an old pro here," I said, not bothering to keep the admiration from my voice.

"This is harder than it looks!" She glanced up and wrinkled her nose. "And what is that smell?"

"The special turtle spa treatment. Guaranteed to remove algae, bacteria, and any other unwanted hitchhikers."

"Smells a little like a bad margarita."

I laughed. "That's the tequila working its magic."

We worked in companionable silence for a few minutes, the only sounds the soft scrubbing of brushes and the occasional scrape of Buster moving a flipper against the plastic pool. He seemed to be in turtle heaven, eyes closed and head drooping.

"He's got quite a dent on this side of his shell," Steph

said, pointing her brush at a deep indentation on Buster's shell, the metal braces still in place. "What happened to him?"

I scrubbed at a stubborn patch of algae, my jaw clenching as I remembered. "He was probably resting on the surface when a boat came by. The propeller did quite a number on him."

"Oh! Poor guy."

"We have a local vet here who used to work at the Turtle Hospital in the Florida Keys. He put the metal plates on Buster's shell to repair it. Worked like a charm."

"I'm glad. And he's living the good life now, at least."

"Yeah," I agreed. "He doesn't have to worry about predators or finding food. Just basking in the sun and getting pampered."

Steph's gaze met mine. "Sounds like my kind of life."

I laughed. "Mine too."

As we worked, our hands brushed occasionally, sending bolts of awareness shooting up my arm. I tried to concentrate on the task at hand, but it was hard with Steph so close. I could smell her shampoo, and I was acutely aware of her every movement—the way her brow furrowed in concentration, and the soft curve of her lips when she smiled.

"Almost done," I said, rinsing the last of the soap suds off Buster's shell.

"He looks brand new." Steph leaned over, inspecting our handiwork. Her fingers brushed mine, and I held my breath, waiting for her to pull away. Instead, she lingered, her touch light but deliberate.

"Thanks for letting me help," she said softly. "It was fun."

"It was a lot more fun with you here," I murmured, my gaze locked on hers.

For a moment, we simply stared at each other, the air between us crackling with unspoken words. Then, as if sensing the shift in the atmosphere, Buster moved one flipper with a loud splash and broke the spell.

Steph drew back with a laugh. "I think someone is ready to go back to his regular digs."

"Okay, big guy," I said, grabbing Buster under his shell. "Time to head back to the penthouse suite."

"Let me help," Steph said, moving to the other side of the kiddie pool.

We lifted Buster together as his legs kicked languidly and carried him back to the big rock pool. After lowering him back into the water, we both let go. As he paddled toward his basking rock, I swore he looked proud of himself. Like he wanted to show off. He moved with a languid grace that belied his bulk, his repaired shell gleaming in the afternoon light.

Sam undulated over to him. He circled around Buster a couple of times, his serpentine body rippling through the water, as the turtle stared nonchalantly at him.

Next to me, Steph grinned. "I think Buster is making that eel jealous!"

That made me laugh. "If you want to give a moray a bath, I'm afraid you're on your own."

"Chicken."

I couldn't keep the goofy smile off my face. "Chicken, or highly skilled in self-preservation. Take your pick."

We turned back to the pool as Sam disappeared back into the shadows, apparently deciding Buster wasn't going to share any secrets.

Her laughter died away, and for a moment our eyes met,

the air between us growing charged. I wanted nothing more than to pull her into my arms and kiss her, right there in the dappled shade of the palm trees.

A trio of laughing guests walked by and jarred us back to reality. Steph rose to rinse her hands at the faucet, and I leaned against a palm tree, my heart thudding against my ribs. I wasn't ready to say goodbye.

"Hey," I said, my voice a little rough, "You want to have dinner?"

"Tonight?" Steph turned off the faucet before straightening and wiped a hand on her damp shorts. "I must look like a swamp monster. I'm covered in turtle gunk."

I grinned, pleased she hadn't turned me down outright. Asking her to dinner was a risk, and I sensed our turtle-scrubbing session might have cleaned the air between us a little. "We both are. Why don't we both go home to clean up and change? I can pick you up at your room. Would an hour be enough?"

A slow smile spread across her face. "An hour will work."

My gaze swept over her, lingering on a smudge of algae near her collarbone. "You always did clean up nice."

Again, we couldn't look away from each other and that current ran between us. Until hesitation flickered through her eyes and she dropped them to the ground. "Will dinner be only... us?"

And just like that, the gulf between us opened again. Reality intruded once more that I was a single father and she lived elsewhere. But dammit, I wasn't ready to give up yet. I couldn't tell whether she wanted Liam to join us or not, but he already had plans. And with him at a sleep over, I might never get a better chance to have dinner with her. "Yes—just us. Liam will be at a friend's." I didn't mention his sleepover, not wanting her to feel pressured. Or set up.

She nodded and the corner of her mouth twitched. "He's a sweet kid, Quinn."

That made me feel better. "Yeah, he is."

My shoulders dropped a little more as her smile steadied. "I need to know what to wear. Do you want to go out somewhere?"

I shook my head. "How about I take you to my house and make you dinner?"

A wide smile creased her face. The smile that had always knocked me flat. "Make me dinner? You can cook?"

"Yes, ma'am." I decided a little flirtation wouldn't hurt. "You'll get to discover some of my talents tonight."

A rush of blood flooded my core when her eyes turned sultry. "With an offer like that, how can I refuse?"

"See you in an hour?"

Her eyes flicked down my body, then back up. "I'll be ready."

As I watched her walk away, my chest was tight with a potent brew of longing and anticipation. As soon as she was out of sight, I grabbed my phone and called my father. "Dad! What did you catch today?"

"Uh... some really nice ahi and a bunch of wahoo."

"Any ahi left?"

"Nope. The restaurants snapped it all up." Bruce Douglas was a career fisherman who had inherited the family business. He was winding things down now that he'd turned sixty.

"Can I have one of the wahoo, then?"

"Sure. We caught several this afternoon that are nice and fresh. Why?"

"I want it for dinner tonight."

A soft laugh echoed over the phone. "Does this have anything to do with Steph being on the island?"

I flinched. "Mom told you, huh? Yes, I invited her over for dinner. That's all. Please don't tell anyone."

Dad's laugh got louder. "You do realize your mother's bridge league was yesterday, don't you? I imagine half of Portsmouth knows already and the rest will know by tonight."

"Great. She's only here for a vacation, Dad!"

"Then why did you mention her to your mother?"

I sighed, knowing a lost cause when I saw one. "I didn't —Mom asked me. Put that fish on ice, will you? I'll pick it up on my way home."

As I rinsed out the kiddie pool and put the cleaning supplies away, my mind was full of the ingredients I'd need to pick up at the market in Portsmouth. I should have time to run everything to my house and straighten up before returning to the Coral Queen to pick up Steph.

A smile cracked my face, excitement about the prospect of a date for the first time in many years. My fingers tingled at the thought that this date was with Steph. I pressed my hand against my hip, imagining it was her soft, porcelain skin instead.

Chapter Twelve

Steph

I CHECKED myself out in the full-length mirror in my room. I had packed a sundress, so I was set for wardrobe. Briefly, I had considered buying something new, but I didn't want to go *too* out of the way. My dress was light green with colorful flowers. It had a fitted bodice that showed plenty of cleavage, and I reconsidered the pink bra and panties I wore underneath.

Should I wear something more modest?

Stop it! I have no idea where this is going, or even where I want it to go. Enough with obsessing!

I'd applied light makeup and curled my hair into small ringlets. Grabbing my hairbrush for the third time, I brushed the curls out yet again, letting my hair hang loose over my shoulders and down my back.

A knock saved me from further ruminations. When I opened the door, Quinn stood there in a fitted black shirt and tan cargo shorts. The shirt, coupled with his almost-black hair, made his eyes stand out even more. I practically salivated at the sight of him. A throb of desire traveled down my body, curling my toes in my sandals.

Quinn's eyes took a slow journey from my head down to my feet, pausing at my breasts. When he met my gaze again, heat smoldered in his eyes. "You look beautiful." His voice was low and throaty. Holding his elbow out to me, he continued with a smile, "Your golf cart awaits."

Laughing, I slid my arm around his and we walked down the hall. In my flat sandals, the top of my head only came to his shoulder. "You look pretty terrific yourself."

He lifted one shoulder. "Glad you think so. I don't own anything too fancy."

As we crossed the lobby, several women's heads behind the front desk turned to follow our progress, confirming my inkling that Quinn didn't date a lot. We entered his golf cart and sped down the main road toward Portsmouth. He turned off just past the market onto a sand road, winding up the small hill that earned this section the tongue-in-cheek moniker of the Heights.

I raised a brow at him. "Moving up in the world, huh?"

"Don't set your expectations too high." He laughed and turned down another sand street. Most of the streets in Portsmouth were made from sand, which was cheap and in plentiful supply.

The neighborhood was made up of modest one and two-story houses with fenced yards. Quinn pulled into an unpaved driveway and parked under a carport. His house was one-story and painted a cheery lavender with white trim.

I exited the cart. "What a cute house!"

Quinn rubbed the back of his neck as he came around the front of the cart and joined my side. We walked toward a glass-paneled door. "I'm renting it from a friend of my mom's. It's small, but it works."

He opened the door—no one in Portsmouth locked theirs—and ushered me into a small kitchen. It was dated but functional and clean. A living room lay behind it with a sectional couch facing a flat-screen television on the wall. Beyond that lay a hallway.

As I studied the home's interior, Quinn crossed the kitchen and opened a cabinet, withdrawing two wine glasses. "You want a glass of wine?"

"Wine?" I grinned at him. "You drink wine now?"

He crossed to the refrigerator and withdrew a bottle of white wine, giving me a flirty smile. "Yes. Believe it or not, I've grown up a little in the past eight years."

"I can see that." I said the words quietly, and our gazes held for a moment, the unspoken message passing between us that I'd recognized he wasn't the same boy I'd broken up with. Quinn produced a waiter's corkscrew and quickly opened the bottle. "I bought a bottle of white and red. White okay to start?"

The Quinn I had known never drank anything but Budweiser, so I was thrilled to accept the glass of Pinot Gris. I took a sip of cool, crisp wine, peach notes teasing my tongue. "This is wonderful."

"Let's sit outside." He ushered me to the living room and through a sliding-glass door leading to a small patio. Placing the wine in a small, dorm-style refrigerator, Quinn invited me to sit at a small patio set. I took in the view as I sat, sipping my wine. His backyard overlooked an expanse of blue, where the darkening blue sky met the turquoise and cobalt water. "You've even got an ocean view!"

He pulled a chair closer and sat down. Our arms were almost, but not quite, touching. "That was my one request when I was looking for a place. I don't really want the upkeep of an oceanfront property, but I need to see the water."

He took a sip of wine, crossing one ankle over his knee. His foot bounced up and down. He saw it and it stilled. Taking a big breath, he met my eyes. "What made you come back to Sandpiper Cay?"

"The same thing as most—a vacation. I've been thinking about diving again for a while, and here I would at least know what I was getting into. And could make sure I didn't dive Slipstream." I took a big drink, settling my nerves, then turned to him again. "Thank you for helping me."

His blue eyes stared back, fine lines at the corners from his time in the sun. "Thank you for letting me. I take it there's no one special in your life?"

I smiled, but it felt sad. "I wouldn't be vacationing alone in a romantic paradise if there were." I shrugged, looking at the ocean. "I broke up with my last boyfriend over a year ago and haven't felt like dating."

"You never married?"

I darted my eyes to his face. His expression was curious, maybe even hopeful. "No, Quinn."

He sighed, his mouth falling into a frown. "And that's something else you can thank me for, I guess."

We were in a good place at the moment. It was time to give a little. "How we ended was devastating. I won't deny that, or that it didn't scar me pretty badly. But you're not the only one who's grown up. I'm a little wiser now too. I pushed you away and expected you'd come running when I snapped my fingers. When that didn't happen, I cut and ran. Not very mature."

"But very understandable. And what happened with Melody wasn't something I could turn my back on. You and

I had already broken up, but her getting pregnant was the real end of us."

I took another sip. My glass was nearly empty, and I stared at the pale fluid, not ready to meet his gaze. My gut tightened. "Quinn, can I ask you something? Something that's eaten at me for years?"

He returned his crossed leg to the ground, leaning forward to place his elbows on his thighs and clasping his hands together. "You can ask me anything, Steph."

Though Quinn had always been devoted, he had never lacked female admirers, on the island or at school in Miami.

"Why Melody? You could have had anyone—why her?"

He briefly closed his eyes, pain etched on his handsome face, then turned fully to me. "Because she was there to give me what I needed. I felt awful about myself. I had no idea what you'd been experiencing behind me on that dive, and you could have died because of it. I thought I was worthless. Melody made me feel otherwise. It was really as simple as that."

"Doesn't sound like a deep, abiding love."

We stared at each other, neither willing to look away.

"It wasn't," he said softly.

My clenched stomach slowly unfurled. "You've been divorced for two years?"

Quinn nodded, relaxing in his chair again. "We shared custody of Liam equally until last summer, when Melody and her boyfriend moved to Destin. I put my foot down and renegotiated our custody agreement. Destin is too far away for joint custody, and she agreed. I keep Liam during the school year, and she gets him over the summer. We'll trade off every other Christmas. I moved back to Sand-piper Cay last fall so my parents could help keep an eye on him."

I gave him a sad smile. "It's closing in on the end of May. School must be over soon."

He cleared his throat thickly and stared at his hands. "Less than two weeks. Soon after, I'll fly him to Destin and hand him over to Melody there."

My heart twisted at the pain on his face. "I'm sorry, Quinn."

He turned a pair of glassy eyes to me, pressing his lips into a thin line. Then he blinked rapidly and took a deep breath. "You don't need to apologize. I've spent the past seven years being the best father I could. I still am. I can't tell you how much I regret how we ended—the pain I caused you. But at least I got Liam out of it. All you got was heartbreak."

"Yet here we are now. Talking about it like two grown adults."

"I'm so sorry, Steph. For everything." He leaned toward me and took my hand in his. His pale eyes had always been expressive, and now they held regret and honest sincerity.

I laced my fingers through his. "So am I. Neither of us was innocent in this, though it took me a long time to recognize my fault. It's much easier to wallow in self-pity and righteous indignation than pull yourself out of it."

A tiny smile raised his lips. "That mean you've successfully dug yourself out?"

"I'm here, aren't I?"

I rubbed my thumb over the back of his hand, acutely conscious of where our skin pressed together. How his fingers were strong and rough—the hands of a man who worked hard for a living. My eyes searched the rugged planes of his face, with his full, parted lips, and my pulse pounded in my ears. Finally, I rested my gaze on his.

Quinn shifted his eyes to my mouth, which felt swollen

with need. "Steph, I really want to kiss you. If you don't want that, now's the time to tell me."

Instead of answering him, I slowly leaned forward. Quinn moved in, wrapping one large hand behind my neck as our lips met. He tasted like crisp white wine, danger, and the ache of eight long years. I tilted my head to the other side of his nose, drawing out the kiss. His lips were warm, yielding softly, though neither of us deepened this first searching contact. It was too fraught with emotion.

The kiss was a simple question. One that both of us answered.

Eventually, Quinn broke away and pressed his cheek to mine. "Thank you for letting me in again."

Then he pulled back and pushed to his feet, retrieved the wine bottle, and refilled our glasses. Strong emotion was written all over his face, a mixture of desire, yearning, and caution. I was curious but was feeling that particular combination myself, so I sat back to let the evening progress as it wanted to.

He gave me a smile, but it looked tight. "I got a fresh wahoo from my dad earlier. I'll get started on dinner."

I watched him leave through the sliding glass door. Was his retreat a sign of things to come? Could this possibly end happily? I sighed and sipped my cold wine, watching the day fade into the ocean.

Neither of us has anywhere else to be right now. Let things play out.

I had hardly taken a drink of wine before Quinn returned to the patio, carrying a long item wrapped in white butcher paper. He opened it to reveal a fish and proceeded to fillet it expertly. That was no surprise. His father was a lifelong fisherman and Quinn had grown up on his boat.

But the meal he made was a revelation. When we'd

been in college, he had struggled with macaroni and cheese. But obviously no longer. He rubbed the fish with blackening spice and grilled it to perfection, adding a twist of lemon. Alongside, he served rice with fresh pineapple chunks mixed in. A garden salad completed the meal.

When he'd asked if I wanted to eat indoors, I shook my head emphatically. "No way. Your view is incredible."

He set an open bottle of red wine on the table, but I nursed my glass of white, not wanting to get too tipsy. A bowl of freshly cut mango sat between us as dessert. "That meal was incredible. Your cooking skills have increased drastically over the years."

Quinn gave me a crooked smile. "Thanks. I was surprised to find out how much I enjoy it."

I ate a chunk of mango, deliciously sweet and tangy. "How long have you been a dive instructor?"

"Three years. Melody and I moved to Fort Lauderdale pretty soon after you left for Tampa. I went into the local dive shop immediately and signed up to take a rescue course. I was determined never to let what you went through happen again. Money was really tight. I'd gotten a job as a longshoreman at the cruise ship docks, but scuba classes aren't cheap. When I found out I could actually make a living as an instructor, I knew that was what I wanted for a career. It took longer than I'd anticipated, but here I am."

"Here you are. You're good at it, Quinn."

"Thanks. So you work for an insurance agency?"

I gave him a quick rundown of my job, aware of how mundane and ordinary it sounded. I'd had visions of being a self-employed entrepreneur in college. But that hadn't happened.

Once again, I found myself opening up to him. That

inexorable call of sharing with someone who knew me so well. "This is the first vacation I've had in two years. Work took over my life, so I got into yoga. I love being the go-to girl in the office, but it's taking a toll on me. I took classes to become a yoga teacher, but I'm stuck in this weird limbo, afraid to make a change." I paused, staring at the distant horizon. "But being here has made me realize I need to. I'll look for a job teaching a class or two on the weekends—dip my foot in a little."

A half-moon played hide-and-seek with the clouds. It streaked from behind a cloudbank, throwing a pale stripe on the ocean. I breathed a long sigh. "It's so peaceful here. I'd forgotten that, how people seem content and happy. I could stare at the ocean all day."

"Don't you do plenty of that in Tampa?"

I smirked. "None. My apartment faces a tree and I work in a high rise with a view of another office building. This is heavenly."

Quinn set his glass down with finality and stood, gathering our dishes. "Come on, then. I know exactly what you need. Let's go for a walk."

I insisted on helping with the dishes since I'd done nothing but sit there while he made dinner. Soon the kitchen was spotless. Quinn crossed to the sectional, lifting a blanket draped over it and folding it over his arm. "Let's go."

"Where are we going?"

"Down to the shore. So you can get your ocean fix." Smiling, he reached out a hand. I took it and we left his house.

As we walked down the sand road, neither of us let go.

Chapter Thirteen

Quinn

STEPH'S HAND was warm and soft inside mine as we walked toward the shore, and I was struck by how natural—how *right*—it felt. I was trying very hard not to make this evening more than it was. Steph had confirmed it over dinner when she'd talked about finding a yoga job after she returned to Tampa. We lived completely separate lives now, with an expanse of ocean and land between us.

What do I want from this?

The answer to that was snug in my wallet. I'd picked up a box of condoms at the market that afternoon and tucked one in my wallet, leaving the others in my nightstand.

Just in case.

It was after 7:00 p.m., and Portsmouth was winding down. It was a working town, not a tourist hotspot. The tourists hung out at Buccaneer Marina. Steph and I passed the marina where my father's and other working boats were moored. We walked along an overgrown path that angled away from the road and soon came to a thick stand of bushes and small trees. I veered into the heavy growth, finally dropping her hand as I tried to clear a path for us.

Steph laughed behind me. "Are you taking me to the Cove?"

"Yeah, though from the looks of it, the Cove doesn't get much use anymore. I think the kids usually hang out at Crescent Beach on the other end of town now." I craned my neck around. Steph was stepping carefully, holding both hands over her head to protect herself from branches and stickers. "You okay? We can go somewhere else. I didn't think this path would be like the damn Amazon."

Her laugh sounded musical, making me smile. "No! Keep going. I want to see what it looks like."

I held up the arm with the blanket folded over it. "You want to hold this over your head? Protect yourself from stickers?"

She grinned as she shook her head. "You're doing a fine job of blazing the trail. I'm keeping my hands up purely for precautionary measures. Lead on, sir."

I did my best to hold the worst of the branches aside for her, and within minutes, we stepped onto a tiny strip of soft white sand. It nearly glowed in the pale moonlight. I stopped, Steph joining my side.

"The beach is smaller than I remember," she said quietly.

"Yeah. Looks like it's eroded some."

The Cove used to be a lovers' lane of sorts. Steph and I had grown up together, but not become romantically involved until our sophomore year at college. We had spent some good times there, a fact that showed in the smile Steph turned to me.

I couldn't resist grinning back. "Come on. I'll lay down the blanket."

I cleaned off a section of sand as best as I could then spread out the soft blanket. We sat side by side, looking out over the hidden cove. Rocks jutted up on either end, making the area extremely private, and no one could penetrate the brush without being heard.

Steph drew her knees up and circled her arms around them. "I feel out of time here. Like only this moment exists."

"Maybe it does," I said, rubbing her back softly. "Maybe that's the key to getting over the past. By focusing on the present."

She turned to me, and moonlight danced in her eyes. She was so beautiful, everything I'd ever wanted in a woman. And I'd lost her. We had so much time to make up for. I reached out and brushed my fingers down the side of her face. "I've really missed you, Steph."

I waited for that guarded expression to enter her eyes, but it didn't. Instead, they warmed further, holding my gaze steadily.

"I've missed you too. I tried to move on, but I never wanted any of the men I dated. Because they weren't you. You were the giant hole in my life no one could fill."

I slid my hand behind her head, pulling her toward me. From the moment our lips met, this kiss was different than the tentative, questioning one we'd shared earlier. Desire rolled through me in a long, powerful wave, sweeping me in its wake.

Closing my fist, I grasped a handful of her silky hair and pulled her head back, giving me better access. I opened my mouth, gently probing. Steph received me eagerly, and my blood caught fire as she moaned softly. Our tongues circled, and I pressed her onto her back, partially rolling on top of her.

Steph slid her hands up the back of my shirt, rubbing

them over every inch of my skin. "My God, Quinn. Did you get these muscles diving?"

I laughed softly. "No. I do plenty of heavy lifting on the job, but most of it is from my home gym."

She tugged at my shirt, lifting it up, and I got the hint. I rose up, ripping my shirt off in one steady motion. Steph's eyes were riveted to my chest as she danced her fingers over my pecs. Blood pulsed through my veins as she pressed her lips to my skin, drawing a wet, slick line from one side of my chest to the other with her tongue.

I was a pulsing, throbbing ball of heat now. "Oh God, Steph."

Attacking her mouth again, I moved one hand to her full breast. Sliding my fingers beneath her dress and bra, I played with the tip, rolling it between my finger and thumb. She arched her back, pressing against my hand, and I smiled against her lips. "Like that, do you?"

"You know I do. I doubt you've forgotten."

I brushed my lips along her jawline and flicked my tongue in her ear. She jumped, and I smiled. "I haven't forgotten anything."

Withdrawing my hand, I stroked it over her side and down her hip, slipping it beneath the hem of her dress. The skin of her thigh was smooth and buttery soft. I fanned my fingers wide as I slowly drew them up her inner thigh.

I crushed my mouth to hers, our teeth smashing together. She breathed in panting gasps as I slid my hand along the top of her panties, then moved beneath. I slid my fingers home. She was warm and very ready, crying out. She kissed me back even harder, nipping at my bottom lip. I groaned, driving my hips against her side, grinding against her.

Steph grabbed my wrist, making me freeze.

"How far are we taking this, Quinn?"

"How far do you want to?"

She pressed against my hand, and I circled my fingers, making her gasp. "I think you know the answer to that."

"I have a condom with me."

She relaxed, and a small smile raised her lips. "I'm very glad to hear that."

Sitting up, she shifted her hips and pulled her dress over her head. I pulled one bra strap off her shoulder and bent my head, running my tongue over her soft skin. In seconds, I had her bra off and tossed it aside. I shucked off my shorts and boxer briefs as she slid her panties off. We stretched out side by side on the blanket.

Her soft, bare body pressing against mine ignited me, my core hot and pulsating. "Oh my God, Steph. I want you so bad."

She took me in her hand and squeezed, laughing softly. "I can see that. I can *feel* that."

I moved to take her breast into my mouth, slowly rolling my tongue in circles. She gasped and ran a hand behind my head, urging me closer. I brushed my fingers down her flat stomach and slid my hand to her inner thigh, pressing her leg out. Steph gave a soft, breathy moan as my fingers reached between her legs, stroking firmly.

I remembered. I knew what this woman liked and wanted. I lifted my head and watched her. Her eyes were closed, her full, flushed lips parted as she moved her hand up and down my shaft.

Climbing on top of her, I trailed my lips to her ribcage and laid a row of kisses to her navel. She had to let go of me, which allowed me to concentrate more fully on her. When I softly nipped her on the abdomen, she cried out, her body convulsing.

I laughed. "I want to hear you louder than that, baby."

She slid her feet up on either side of my hips, bending at the knees, and swept both hands over my shoulders. "I'm on fire right now."

Not yet, but you will be...

In one fast movement, I climbed down and took a long taste of her. She was nearly ready to climax anyway—all her signals came back to me instantly. I swirled my tongue, probing and focusing on every moan and shiver coming from her. Her hands pressed against the back of my head as she cried out into the tropical night.

When Steph finally relinquished her hold, I sat up on my knees and withdrew my wallet from my shorts. I quickly found the condom and rolled it on. Slowly, teasingly, I kissed my way back up her luscious body, lingering once more on her breasts.

This time her moan held a twinge of frustration as she tugged on my shoulders. "Come here. I need you now."

Happy to oblige, our lips came together as, at last, I eased my way inside her. A deep, throaty groan rushed from my lungs as I was enveloped by her warmth, and sheer sensation rolled through me as I started moving above her.

We fit together perfectly. We always had.

Steph wrapped her legs around my waist, sending me even deeper.

"Oh God, Steph. This is amazing."

She pulled my mouth back to hers, plunging her tongue in, and wrapped her arms tightly around me. As I thrust in even deeper, she moved her hands to my shoulders and pushed me off, rolling on top.

We never even disturbed our rhythm. Or our kiss.

Eventually, Steph sat up, and the moon lit her breasts as she arched her back. The sight was almost too much, and I sat up before her, wrapping both arms around her and pulling her tight. The sensation of coming home again was undeniable, inexorable. At last, I completely let go within the storm building inside, rising and engulfing me.

As I lay back down, my heart slowed to its usual rhythm. A gentle breeze cooled my sweaty chest, and Steph ran her hands over it, raising goosebumps. She smiled and folded over me as I gathered my arms around her. I pressed my lips to her hair, closing my eyes and drowning willingly in the emotion overcoming me. "Welcome home, Steph."

Chapter Fourteen

Steph

QUINN'S ALARM clock went off, an insistent, repetitive beeping that made me screw up my face. Behind me, he fumbled loudly, making slapping sounds until the alarm abruptly went quiet. Then he scooted toward me, wrapping his large body behind mine. His warmth surrounded me, and I never wanted to get out of bed. I cracked an eye and stared blearily at my watch. My sleepy contentment got a rude awakening. "You set your alarm for six a.m.?"

He snuggled closer, pressing his lips against the back of my neck. "Mmm-hmm. Mornings are usually pretty hectic."

Resisting a smile, I tried again. "Six a.m.? I'm on vacation, Quinn."

"Good for you. I'm not."

Finally breaking into a grin, I dug my elbow into his side, earning a solid, deep laugh from behind. Last night, we'd strolled back to his house and ended up in his bedroom. Neither had had much sleep, not that I was complaining. And from the stiffness steadily growing against my lower back, I didn't think falling back asleep now was on the table either.

He reached around and stroked my breast. "We don't have to get up quite yet if you don't want..."

"What happened to vaulting out of bed to tackle your hectic morning?"

He pressed against me. "You happened."

Happiness flushed through my body, tickling the bottoms of my feet. "Well, that is a very good answer." I rolled over and pressed the length of my body against his.

Half an hour later, I took a quick shower while Quinn made coffee. Twirling my wet hair into a bun, I walked into the kitchen, once again wearing my sundress. Quinn poured coffee into two mugs. He was dressed for work in a Coral Quest T-shirt and board shorts. A gallon of milk and a bag of sugar sat on the counter. "You still take cream and sugar in your coffee?"

"No sugar, but milk is good."

I added a splash and took a sip. Last night we had melted together like we were made for each other. The sex had been better than when we'd been together before. Then again, we were older now.

But the night was over, and I would be leaving Sandpiper Cay soon. Though I meant to guard my heart carefully, my body was having a grand old time. Especially with Quinn standing right next to me, giving off those man vibes.

"You diving this morning?" he asked.

I shook my head. "My ears are a little sore. Along with some other parts."

His fallen expression at hearing my first sentence

turned to a sly, self-satisfied grin at my second. "Maybe they need a little rest this morning."

I laughed softly. "They've had quite a workout. But I'll dive tomorrow morning."

Quinn widened his eyes in mock innocence. "Oh? Are we talking about diving? I'd forgotten."

"Ha-ha. Maybe I'll stop by the marina and visit you today."

His expression softened. "I'd like that."

Crossing to the table to pick up my phone, which I hadn't looked at since the previous evening. I groaned at the half dozen text messages. All were from my friend Jana, each text escalating in desperation as she sought help for our new work project. The final one had been sent fifteen minutes prior.

> Jana: I know you're on vacay and all that. But are you ghosting me? You wouldn't do that, would you????

I exhaled a long sigh. "Great. Looks like I've got a work emergency to deal with." I quickly answered.

> Steph: No, I'm not ghosting you! I'll call within an hour, okay?

"You want me to give you a lift back to the Coral Queen?" Quinn asked as he poured coffee into a travel cup. "I've got a little time before I have to pick up Liam from his friend's."

"Thanks, that would be great."

Hearing Liam's name brought home the fact that as at ease as we'd been last night, we were different people now. I had enjoyed the few minutes I'd spent with Liam and wanted to know him better.

Maybe we can have dinner together before I go.

But I didn't want to bring up the idea while we were both still dancing around each other in the morning-after ballet. And now that reality had reappeared, I was craving some distance. I needed perspective.

Fifteen minutes later, Quinn pulled to a stop under the covered landing of the Coral Queen. Turning toward me, he ran his hand softly over my shoulder. "I'm glad we got together last night."

My smile turned mischievous. "Yeah, I could tell."

He brushed a finger down the bridge of my nose. "I'm serious."

My smile faded as his eyes held me. I couldn't look away, even if I wanted to. Which I didn't. "I know. I'm glad too."

Quinn quickly leaned forward, smashing his lips hard against my mouth. His kiss wasn't what I had expected—it was searching, demanding, almost like he wanted to put his stamp on me. When he pulled away, his chest moved up and down with his hard breathing. "I'll see you later, okay?"

My blood sang as it coursed through my veins. When I opened my mouth, my voice came out as a squeak. I cleared my throat and tried again. "Yes."

Tearing my eyes away from his, I stepped out of the golf cart, locking my knees to keep from stumbling. I didn't look back, afraid I wouldn't be able to walk away a second time.

I crossed the lobby, my mind full of Quinn, of the feel of his hard body under my hands. All those muscles! He had been familiar, yet completely new. I couldn't get enough of him last night.

Oh yeah. And this morning too. No wonder I'm sore!

Work was probably a good thing. I needed a distraction.

After shutting the door to my room, I dug my phone out and dialed Jana. "Okay. What's the emergency?"

"I'm really sorry, Steph! I tried so hard not to bother you. But I'm looost."

Despite my irritation, a smile arose, picturing my friend and her short brown curls. Jana always had a flair for the dramatic.

"Lost about what?"

"The new account! The spreadsheets! Sooo many spreadsheets."

"Deep breaths, Jana. What *specifically* do you need help with?"

"Um... well, here's the thing. There's a small problem with the master customer list."

I tossed my key card on the dresser and slipped out of my sandals. "I'm listening."

"It's gone."

"What do you mean, 'it's gone'?"

"Steph, I told you I couldn't do this without you! I'm hopeless at spreadsheets. I'm supposed to do the calculations, remember?"

A cold ball formed in my gut. "What happened to the list?"

"I don't knoooow!"

I refrained from smashing my head against the door. "Can you be more specific?"

"I think I deleted it accidentally. I opened it, did something with another file, then I couldn't find it again. Roger is going to fire me for sure!"

Roger was our boss and well acquainted with Jana's theatrics. Which wouldn't prevent him from terminating her if she really screwed up. But I wasn't too worried. "I'm sure it's still there. You probably just turned on a filter or something. What were you working on?'

"I was organizing the customers by county."

"Eminently sensible, with hurricane season coming up."

"Can you find the file for me? I've got a meeting with Roger at noon, and I have to have all those files updated."

"What? You want me to do this now? While I'm on vacation?"

"I'll make it up to you! I promise. Drinks, dinner, whatever you want."

"Jana, what I want is to lie on the beach with a Purple Passion in my hand."

"Ooh, if it's attached to a man, I want to hear more."

I burst out laughing, and the words tumbled out of my mouth. "I did have a rather amazing night last night."

"Oh my God! Now I really want to hear more. But I need that file! I know you brought your laptop... you always do."

My eyes drifted to the desk in my room, my laptop sitting square on the surface. "Jana..."

"Come on. It won't take you any time at all. I'm sure you can find the lost file and organize all the contacts in like five minutes."

"What? Now you want me to do the county separations too?"

"I still have preliminary figures to finalize before the meeting. You should feel guilty—leaving me with all this!"

I raised a hand to my brow and broke into reluctant laughter. "Okay, fine. You win. I'll log onto the server and get this done. I'll let you know when I'm finished."

"You're the best! And I want a full rundown on your amazing night, okay?"

. . .

IT TOOK LONGER than I expected. After changing into clean clothes, I ordered a room service breakfast and nibbled on it as I tried to unravel the knot. Jana *had* actually deleted the master subscriber list. Somehow. Fortunately, I always maintained backups on my private work drive and was able to restore the file. Separating the customers by county was tedious, though not difficult. But it was still a big job.

At 10:00 a.m., Jana sent a text asking how it was going. I replied curtly.

> Steph: it will go faster if I'm not interrupted.

Then Jana texted at eleven, asking for another update. I rubbed my eyes—I needed a little break anyway.

> Steph: I'm in the home stretch. I'll have it done for your meeting with Roger.

> Jana: Thanks! You're the best.

I typed my response and sent it before I could second-guess myself, grinning.

> Steph: That's what he said. LOL.

> Jana: Arghh! We don't have time to chat before my meeting. I NEED DETAILS.

> Steph: I'm trying to keep you from getting fired, remember? I need to get back to it.

I finished the project with fifteen minutes to spare, emailed the updated files to Jana, and wished her good luck with her meeting. Then it occurred to me that the morning dive trip returned to the dock around noon every day.

My eyes wandered to the clear turquoise water visible outside my slider. *I said I'd try to track him down today. But can I just enjoy a vacation fling with Quinn? Without wanting more?*

Only time would answer that question.

The day had become hot and sultry. I met a group of divers walking along the brick pathway, an anticipatory flurry running through me. When I stepped onto the wooden dock at Buccaneer Marina, I nodded at Diego, who smiled as he pushed a cart of scuba tanks toward the dive shop.

Quinn was still on board, talking to a woman. He stood casually, one hip cocked, but my gaze narrowed on the woman in front of him. About our age, she gave a coy laugh I heard halfway down the dock. The woman twisted her hair over one shoulder, eyeing Quinn appreciatively.

Jealousy shot through me like a lance, stopping me in my tracks as my body screamed, *Mine! He's mine!*

Shocked at my reaction, I studied Quinn. I couldn't see his face, but his body language reflected friendly professionalism. He wasn't leaning toward the woman and said something quietly. Her sultry expression faltered. A grim, satisfied smile rose on my face.

The woman gave Quinn a quick nod and hurried off *Aqua Dreams*, hunching her shoulders. She passed me without looking up. On board, Quinn rolled his head around on his neck before slinging a BCD over his shoulder. He hopped onto the wooden dock, heading away from me and toward the room where they stored scuba gear.

My body was like a heat-seeking missile, determined to stake a claim on him, despite what my mind—or heart—kept trying to tell it. I took off at a deliberate pace down the dock. When I reached the wooden shed, Quinn was placing the BCD on its hanger.

"Another boatload of satisfied divers?" I asked, my voice low and husky.

Quinn turned around and the smile that slid over his face made my skin tingle from head to toe. Desire radiated off him—*very* different from his posture with the woman who had just left. "I'm not sure. One very important diver was missing. Kind of threw a damper on the whole morning."

I sauntered over, and Quinn's eyes slowly traveled down my body, then back up. His eyes were positively molten. A hot lance rocketed down my body. Stopping in front of him, I stroked a finger down his broad chest. "It wouldn't be right if you had too much fun without me, now would it?"

Quinn grabbed my ponytail and yanked my head back. Bending his neck, he smashed his lips into mine. He parted my lips with his tongue, spearing it into my mouth as he grabbed my ass. I met him fully and wrapped one leg around his hip. Using both hands, I riffled my fingers through his hair, clenching my hands. I pulled him even tighter against my mouth, earning myself a deep, tight groan from Quinn.

Smiling against his lips, I unwound my leg and pressed both hands against his chest, walking him backward. The BCD he'd hung crashed to the floor. I growled, a deep, primal sound as I explored the inside of his mouth. He slipped one hand around to grab my breast, squeezing hard as he groaned into my mouth.

Didn't act like this around that other woman, did you, Quinn? Only I do this to you.

The flush of triumph, of certainty, gave me even greater pleasure as I ran my hands over his thick forearms and up to his shoulders.

Suddenly, he broke the kiss and took a big step back, panting. "God, Steph. What are you doing to me?"

I reached down and squeezed him, not surprised to find him rock-hard. "The same thing you're doing to me. Just by being near you."

"I'm half a minute from taking you right here and now. To hell with whoever walks in."

"Does the door have a lock?"

As he shook his head, voices drifted toward us, pulling us both back to reality. Quinn darted his eyes toward the open doorway, then back to mine. He shot me a lopsided smile. "We can't get caught in here feeling each other up."

I laughed quietly. "I guess that wouldn't be very professional, would it? What would you suggest?"

"I'm teaching a class this afternoon. How about I come up to your room after? Around three o'clock?"

I could think of a hundred reasons why that was a bad idea, but none of them seemed important. Right now, the only important thing was the man in front of me. I swore he was giving off pheromones. Lust came off him in waves, nearly overpowering me. Consequences could wait until later.

I nodded, my chest moving with each deep breath. "I'll be waiting. Hurry."

Chapter Fifteen

Quinn

I HELD Steph against my chest, stroking the soft skin on her back, damp with sweat. Light illuminated the edges of her closed blinds, and I pulled up the sheet to cover her. I blinked rapidly, forcibly keeping my eyes open. Which wasn't easy after yet another amazing physical session together. I didn't have time for a nap.

All morning I'd tried to convince myself that our chemistry the previous night had been a fluke, part of that strange moment out of time. But when Steph showed up in the gear room, there was no denying our attraction. And the fluke theory was completely demolished now. We had clawed each other's clothes off as soon as I entered her room, and now were both totally sated. Relaxing in each other's arms.

I really needed to get going.

Instead, I tilted Steph's chin up and bent my head to kiss her.

She made a satisfied hum and stretched against me. "We weren't this good together before."

"No. We're both older now. More experienced."

She frowned. "I'm not promiscuous, you know."

I twitched one side of my mouth. "I never meant to insinuate you were. I've only been with two women since you, Steph. But eight years is a long time."

"I've been in two relationships since, too. But what you and I have together... it's different."

"I know." I also knew the clock was ticking on our reunion. Which reminded me of the time, and I glanced at my watch. "I need to go. I have to pick up Liam from Mom and Dad's."

"She watches him a lot?"

"For a few hours after school almost every day. I'd be sunk without her."

"Your mom loves kids. I'm sure she enjoys it."

"She does, and he adores her."

Get moving, man.

Tossing back the sheets, I padded to the bathroom to dispose of the condom and redress. When I returned, Steph sat propped up on the pillows, the sheet tucked over her breasts. I sat down next to her and cupped her face before pressing a soft kiss to her lips. "See you on the dive boat tomorrow."

"I'll be there. Have a good night."

We broke eye contact, an awkwardness filling the silence. I rose and walked out the door.

Back to my life.

WHEN I ENTERED MY PARENTS' house, my mother stood at the sink rinsing dishes while Liam kicked a soccer ball in the backyard.

I gave her a one-armed hug, making her smile. "How

was work today?"

"Fine. We saw a white tip shark, which was unusual."

"I'm sure that made the divers happy. Was Steph there?" Her tone was casual but didn't fool me for a second. I could practically see her nose twitching with anticipation.

"No. A work emergency came up and she had to spend the morning sorting it out."

"Oh. Did you two have a nice evening?"

I couldn't resist a small smile as I placed a plate in the dishwasher. "Yeah, we did. I think we both got some more perspective on what happened before."

Mom's brows rose. "And what does that mean?"

"It means we went out on a date and enjoyed each other's company," I said, not about to get into details with my *mother*. "We didn't get bogged down in the past. But Steph lives in Tampa, and I live here. She'll leave soon, and I doubt we'll ever see each other again."

Mom tossed her hand towel on the counter. "Why, Quinn? Maybe you two owe it to yourselves to see if you really have moved beyond what happened."

Steeling myself, I shook my head as I rinsed a casserole dish. "My priority is Liam. He's been through a lot in the past year, and he needs stability from me."

Mom stilled, looking me square in the eye. "And what do you need, son?"

That is a very good question. "I'm not sure. But it's not a long-distance relationship. I know that much." I sighed, then gave my mother a tiny smile. "I know you've always loved Steph, Mom. But I'm not at all sure how she'd feel being around Liam. That's got to be tough for her. Don't get your hopes up, okay?"

"I only want you to be happy. And you never were with Melody. That was obvious. I can understand how seeing

Liam might upset Steph, but don't underestimate her." She patted my arm, then closed the dishwasher. "I'm helping Grace Horvath tomorrow afternoon with her bake sale. Can I drop Liam off at the dive shop after school?"

"Of course. He loves hanging out there." I opened the back door and walked onto the lawn, where Liam and I kicked the soccer ball around. My troubled love life faded into the back of my mind as I concentrated on my son.

Chapter Sixteen

Steph

A SWEET-SCENTED AFTERNOON breeze washed over my face as I sat on my balcony. It was 5:00 p.m., which meant Jana should be home, and I picked up my phone.

Jana was breathless when she answered. "So have you been sipping cocktails on the beach all afternoon with Tall, Dark, and Handsome?"

I laughed. "One out of two. The man I was with pretty much invented that phrase. But we didn't spend our time on the beach."

"Ooh! Juicy. Tell me all about him. Is he visiting from some far off, exotic land?"

"Just the opposite. He lives on Sandpiper Cay. You ready for a shock?"

Jana paused for a moment. "Really? You're having a fling with a local, huh?"

"I'm having a fling with Quinn." I hadn't known Jana in college, but as my best friend, she knew all about him.

"Wait. What? The guy who ruined your life? He Who Must Not Be Named?"

"I had no idea Quinn would be here! We got off to a pretty rocky start, but he's a dive instructor now and got me back in the water."

"You went there specifically to dive again, so I guess that makes sense." Jana spoke slowly, like she was trying to put the pieces together. "Though I'm not sure how diving leads to falling into bed together."

"I'm still figuring that out too. But it's been a long time, and we've both grown up."

Jana blew a long sigh. "Steph, I'm having a hard time with this. You taught me to hate this guy, remember?"

I laughed ruefully. "Yeah, I know. But I broke up with him, not the other way around. He didn't cheat on me."

"No. He just got some other chick you couldn't stand knocked up right away. I take it they broke up?"

"They're divorced now."

"Ahhh. The plot thickens. So, are we talking a little vacation fun here, or something more?"

That was the million-dollar question. I stared at the swaying palm trees, not really seeing them. "Depends on what part of my body is answering that question. My head is saying to have my fun and go back to Tampa. Leave Quinn behind. But, man. My body is saying something completely different."

"Was the sex *that* good?"

"Better. And if I'm being honest, it's more than that. He made me dinner last night, and we had a really good time talking again."

"He made you dinner? Like hot dogs or something?"

I burst into laughter. "No! Like blackened fresh-caught

fish. He's a really good chef, which is definitely a change from the old Quinn."

"Hmmm. So he's gorgeous, has an exotic job, and can cook? I see your dilemma now."

"Thank you!"

"What about the kid?"

Liam's face flashed into my mind. "He has custody of his son during the school year. I met him, and he's the spitting image of Quinn."

"How did you feel about that?"

"I was pretty shocked at first. But he's a very sweet boy. Then Quinn came across us and his eyes practically bulged out of his head. He whisked his son away. I got the feeling Quinn hadn't intended for us to meet."

"You haven't talked about this with him?"

"Not really. We had plenty of other subjects to discuss. What's the point, if we're going our separate ways in a few days?"

"True. But if Quinn doesn't want you around his son, that's a pretty major stumbling block. I wonder why he rushed the boy away."

"I think he was being protective."

Jana breathed a long, dreamy sigh through the phone. "Now we have to add protective single father to the list of positives. You'd better come up with some negatives, Steph, or you could be in trouble here."

Don't I know it. "The negative is that we live completely different lives. And you're right. He did ruin my life."

"Did he, though? You broke up with him."

"Whose side are you on?"

Jana laughed. "You said it yourself. A lot of time has passed."

I stretched out my legs and crossed one ankle over the other. "True, but there was a lot of heartache. On both sides. Quinn and Liam are a package deal, and there's no doubt about it."

"Is that okay with you?"

My eyes drifted to several children playing in the pool below. "I love kids. I'd like some of my own. And what happened between Quinn and me certainly wasn't Liam's fault."

"He's called Liam?" Jana squealed. "What an adorable name!"

"Yeah, it is. But I'm not thinking ahead of tomorrow. I'm going diving in the morning in Quinn's group. Then we'll see what the rest of the day brings."

"Well, it hasn't been a boring vacation. At least you can say that."

"Yeah. Just like I can say I had to work during it."

"I'm sorry! I really am. But you're so good at this stuff."

My gaze took in the turquoise water and palm trees outside. That was the problem. I *was* good at my job. The job that was feeling more and more like a noose around my neck. In college, I'd been on fire with ideas of starting my own small business. Then Quinn had crushed me—and my confidence—and I'd retreated into safety. Where I'd stayed ever since.

Monica's offer of the yoga instructor position intruded on my thoughts again, but I didn't mention it to Jana. I hardly wanted to mention it to myself.

One step at a time...

Chapter Seventeen

Steph

THE NEXT MORNING, I found myself buddied up with the woman who'd been flirting with Quinn the previous day. We were the only single divers aboard *Aqua Dreams*, so it made sense, and Quinn hadn't acted anything but completely professional when he introduced us.

I never told him I saw her flirting with him. Or that he shut her down fast.

Remembering our quick reunion in the gear room—where Quinn had acted completely differently—made me feel magnanimous toward the woman, whose name was Britt. She looked about my age, with long dark hair she pulled into a low ponytail.

She smiled at me. "Morning. Looks like we're the two singles on the trip."

I inspected my gear. Everything looked ship-shape. "Fine by me. It'll be fun."

Britt's eyes slid to Quinn, who was chatting with an older couple. His sunglasses sat propped on his head, and he wore a light-blue staff polo shirt. She sighed, a wistful expression on her face. "With him around, definitely. I'm not sure he's single, though. I tried to chat him up yesterday, but he wasn't real receptive."

I drank him in as memories of our previous afternoon in my room came flooding back. As if he sensed my gaze, Quinn's eyes shifted to me. An easy, slow smile rose on his face that made me weak in the knees.

Britt burst into laughter as she alternated her gaze between us. "Wow! That was *not* the reaction I got. I take it you two know each other?"

"Yeah, but it's been a long time."

Quinn strolled our way, moving with a casual confidence that made everything else around me fade away. "Hello again," he said. "You two getting to know each other?"

"We are," I replied, trying to come back to earth. "I'm looking forward to the dives."

"The first site isn't far, so you guys might want to start getting ready now." As Quinn walked toward Captain Sam, he casually brushed my hand. An electric shock ran through me.

"A long time, huh?" Britt asked, raising a brow. "Doesn't look like it."

"We've reconnected since I've been here. I need to get my wetsuit." Not eager to discuss my nascent love life, I got ready to dive.

That morning's dives felt very different than those I'd completed only forty-eight hours prior. Because Quinn and I were different. Instead of imagining what was under his wetsuit, I was intimately acquainted with every inch of his body. And I was very different—more assured in my skills and able to enjoy the experience more.

He still checked on me often, and my confidence grew in leaps and bounds. I realized Quinn was selecting our dive sites carefully to rebuild my belief in myself, but it was working. *We* were working. He came over to chat with Britt and me during our surface interval between dives, and we fell into an easy camaraderie. It left me wondering if a long-distance relationship might be possible after all.

Could this really work out—Quinn and me after all these years?

After we returned to Buccaneer Marina, he was thronged by divers asking questions, so I slipped off the boat and headed back to my room. We hadn't made any plans to see each other again, but I wasn't concerned. We had each other's numbers.

I showered and changed into a breezy yellow sundress, then headed down to lunch. I ate alone but recognized several divers and waved to them. After eating, Fuchsia Flow called my name, and I strolled over. Monica was in the middle of a class, so I checked the schedule. An advanced class was scheduled for that afternoon, and I signed up for it, excited to get back to yoga.

With no particular destination in mind, I wound around the pool deck, and my feet took me toward Coral Quest. Buster was resting in the shallows, his repaired shell out of the water and a much lighter color when dry. I sat on the rocky edge of the pool, watching several blue tangs swimming around. Buster raised his head out of the water and peered at me for a long moment. But when I didn't move, he ducked it underwater again and closed his eyes.

I grinned. *You've got a nice life here, don't you?*

The front door of the dive shop opened, drawing my attention. Liam walked out, struggling to carry a white five-gallon bucket with both arms. My heart nearly stopped, then resumed at a faster pace. I stood as he shuffled around the pool. "Do you need some help carrying that?"

He looked up, widening his eyes in surprise. "No, thanks. I've got it. I'm used to carrying this." Liam set the bucket, half filled with water, down near me. Several pieces of sponge Quinn had located on our dive lay at the bottom.

"Lunch time for Buster?"

"It's a little late to be lunch, but I don't think he cares."

Liam sat down and fished out a long piece of sponge. As soon as he sat down, Buster swam over. I studied Liam out of the corner of my eye. He was so like Quinn! But where Quinn might have been carved from granite, his son was chiseled from fine porcelain, his features still fresh and round.

"Buster sure knows who you are!" I said with a laugh as the turtle gently took the food from Liam's hand.

The boy handed me a piece of the reddish-brown sponge. "Yeah. We're pretty good friends." He glanced at me, curiosity flickering in his blue eyes. "My dad said you used to be friends with him."

I made sure not to react, though I was surprised Quinn had said anything to Liam about me. "A long time ago, when we were in college. But I live in Tampa now. I'm on Sandpiper Cay for a vacation."

Buster finished his sponge, and I held mine out. The door to the dive shop opened again, but I was making sure the turtle got his treat and didn't look up.

"Steph... hello."

Brenda Douglas's voice made me freeze, causing Buster to swim forward to grab the sponge from my outstretched hand. Quinn's mother looked little different, except her hair was grayer now.

I stood and smiled tentatively. "Hi, Brenda."

Liam watched us closely as the older woman darted her eyes all over my body. "You look lovely, dear. It's so wonderful to see you again."

"You, too. It's been an interesting trip back."

Brenda's eyes filled with warmth and something more. Sympathy. "Yes. I imagine it has."

I had been close to Quinn's parents and was genuinely interested in them. "How have you and Bruce been?"

"Good. He's still captaining a fishing boat, and I'm mostly at home. I help on volunteer projects now and again but stay plenty busy."

I wasn't surprised. Quinn's mother had always been a ball of energy. "Do you come to the dive shop often?"

Brenda laughed, the slightly awkward atmosphere breaking. "No. I was dropping Liam off." She narrowed her eyes, watching me closely. I made sure to keep my face expressionless. "I watch him after school most days, but today I'm helping a friend with a project. Which reminds me—" She checked her watch. "I need to get going." She turned to Liam, who stood to give her a hug. "See you tomorrow, sweetie."

"Bye, Grandma."

As he sat and fed Buster, Brenda turned to me. "I'm glad we ran into each other. Enjoy your stay."

"I will. Good to see you again."

With a nod, Brenda moved to step around me, then suddenly stopped to wrap her arms tightly around me.

I was startled but hugged Quinn's mother back, a reminder of times gone by.

"I've missed you," Brenda whispered, then hurried away without waiting for a response.

I stared at her retreating back, then turned around to

find Quinn in front of me. His guarded expression told me he'd seen the embrace.

"Hi," he said, his voice stiff, all traces of our earlier intimacy gone.

"Hello. It was nice to see your mother again."

Quinn's expression softened, a smile breaking out. "She always thought you hung the moon. I'm sure she was thrilled."

I smiled back. "You're lucky to have her so close."

"I am." He turned to his son, who was watching the exchange openly. "I'm finished up. Why don't you go back inside and gather your things?"

"Okay." Liam glanced at me, curiosity lighting up his eyes. "You can feed Buster the rest of the sponges if you want."

"Thanks! I'll do that." As Liam skirted the pool, I turned back to Quinn. "You have a wonderful son. I like him a lot."

"He's pretty easy to like. And thank you." The tight, guarded expression was back, giving me an idea.

If we're going to have a shot as a couple, we need to start somewhere. "Why don't we have dinner tonight?"

Quinn's face went blank. "I can't have dinner with you. I've got Liam."

"So? Bring him too. I'd love to get to know him better."

He raked a hand through his hair, frustration tightening his rugged features. "No, Steph. I'm not going to confuse him by introducing him to you."

My body stiffened, my stomach twisting. "We already know each other. How would that confuse him?"

Quinn stared at me, his eyes narrowed, and his jaw set tight. "Steph, his mother moved away and left him. They still talk regularly, but Liam's had a rough time adjusting to not seeing her for months. I can't introduce another woman who's only going to be here a few days. I won't do that to him."

I took a step back, tears filling my eyes.

Serves me right for thinking with my heart instead of my head! Why did I think things could be different?

I lifted my chin and straightened, trying to blink away the wetness in my eyes. "I'm sorry I asked. I'm not out to hurt your son, Quinn. I only wanted to have a casual dinner. Good night." Spinning on my heel, I hurried away. The tears overflowed, spilling down my cheeks.

"Steph! Wait... I didn't mean that how it came out."

Wiping a furious hand over my cheek, I stopped and whirled around. "No, Quinn. I think you meant exactly what you said."

When I turned around the second time, he didn't try to stop me.

Chapter Eighteen

Quinn

I WATCHED STEPH STALK AWAY, at a loss for words. I'd never been a smooth talker, and the last thing I wanted to do was hurt her. Again. Yet my words had come out all wrong.

Dammit! I'm only trying to protect Liam. Why did I do such a shitty job of explaining that?

I was debating going after her stiff retreating form when Liam pushed through the door of Coral Quest, ending that train of thought.

Gonna have to fix things with Steph later.

I rested my hand on Liam's shoulder as we walked to the golf cart. He snuck glances at me the whole way, ending any question I had that Liam knew something was going on between Steph and me.

As we drove down the access lane, Liam spoke. "Your friend left while I was in the dive shop?"

"Yes. She's not really a friend, though."

"Grandma seemed to like her. How come you're not friends anymore?"

I tapped my fingers on the steering wheel. *How do I answer that?* "We were close in college but went our separate ways. Until a few days ago, we hadn't talked in years."

Liam wasn't fooled. "How close?"

"She was my girlfriend. Before your mom."

"Oh. She seems nice."

I watched Liam out of the corner of my eye. He looked straight ahead and showed no signs of unease. I hadn't been on a date since moving to Sandpiper Cay months ago. Until Steph. This was a good time to test the waters with Liam. "How would you feel if I had a girlfriend?"

Liam turned to me, both brows raised, then shrugged. "I don't know. I've never thought about it."

I pulled over to the side of the road, coming to a full stop. I gripped the passenger headrest with my right hand, giving Liam my full attention. "I want you to know you're my first priority. I know this last year has been really hard, and I don't want to do anything to upset you."

"It was weird when Mom started seeing Craig. But he's nice to me and I got used to it." Liam cocked his head. "Does this mean you want Steph to be your girlfriend?"

Son, that's the million-dollar question. Though I might have just blown it with her permanently. "Not necessarily. I was asking in general terms."

"You both scuba dive, though."

I smiled. "Yeah, we've got quite a few things in common. But she lives in Tampa, not here."

Liam frowned. "Does that mean you'd move to Tampa?"

"No," I answered immediately. "I won't uproot you again when you've finally gotten settled here. Sandpiper Cay is our home."

"Good," Liam said, his smile returning. "I like it here.

Maybe I'll become a dive instructor like you when I grow up."

I pulled back onto the road. "You definitely could. But I thought you were going to be a professional soccer player."

"Well, I need a backup plan in case I get hurt. If that happens, I'll be a dive instructor."

I grinned. *God, I love this kid.* "Is that right? Dive instructor isn't good enough for you, huh?" I poked Liam in the side until he broke into giggles.

As I made dinner, my mind kept returning to Steph. I chopped up bell peppers for the stir fry, remembering how easily we'd gotten over our initial awkwardness. And her hostility. How I'd been lulled back into being with her. Being *us* again.

Until I'd seen her with Liam once more, and reality had stormed in.

During our dive that morning, I'd caught myself having fantasies about the two of us diving on my days off. She'd made remarkable progress, and her enjoyment was obvious. And I'd forgotten how comfortable I was around Steph. It had all come back the past two days. How good we were.

Were.

But we were completely different people now. Living very different lives. And my words that afternoon as I attempted to protect Liam might have ended any speculation over where we might have gone.

Over the evening, I sent Steph several texts that went unanswered.

I wanted to make up for that terrible dive that drove us apart. And I have. So why am I still pursuing her?

Because we weren't finished yet.

Steph had unloaded her anger at me and given me the chance to make up for it. Except there was more. More buried under the guilt I'd always felt about how we ended, and the look on Steph's face when I'd told her about Melody being pregnant. Beneath all that, I had always been upset—even angry—over the fact that I had ended up as the bad guy in the breakup. That I hadn't suffered as a result too. One dive had changed the course of my entire life and all the plans I'd had.

Maybe Steph and I needed to have one final conversation and get closure. End things once and for all, then go our separate ways.

So why did that thought cause an open, gaping hole in my stomach?

Chapter Nineteen

Steph

I SAT in my room and stared at the wall, still in a daze. *How could I have been so dumb to get sucked in again?*

The thing was, I was pretty sure it wasn't just me. When Quinn saw me with Liam again, his eyes hadn't only held that protective, guarded look. Shock had been there too. Like he'd gotten slapped with reality as much as I had. We'd been in a bubble, only the two of us again.

But it wasn't just us anymore.

Quinn had to consider Liam now, and I understood that. I frowned at the framed sandpiper print on the wall.

It's not like I'm out to replace his mother or trying to hurt him. I like how protective Quinn is, but he's going overboard.

Then again, I wasn't a mother. Let alone a parent of a little boy whose life had been turned upside down. I sighed and stood, stretching my arms over my head. *I'm being judgy again.*

But what did it matter? I was going home in a few days.

A ten-day vacation had seemed like an extravagant

expanse of time when I'd arrived, but my time was flying by. My trip was more than half over.

It was time for the class I'd signed up for. After changing into stretchy leggings matched with a fitted tank top, I headed to Fuchsia Flow. And once again, yoga worked its magic on me, especially since this was an advanced class. Only one other woman was in attendance, and I worked up a sweat. Monica taught a challenging class, including several handstand poses, and it was exactly what I needed.

Distraction, relaxation, motion.

I worked hard on my handstand tree pose but couldn't do it one-handed without losing my balance. *Guess I'm not as at peace as I thought.*

After the class, I disinfected my mat and placed it back in the bin. Checking my phone, there were several text messages from Quinn. I ignored them.

"I haven't seen you lately," Monica said, stopping next to me. "I thought you might have returned home."

"I leave in a few more days."

"Does that mean you spent the last couple of days with Quinn?"

"Yes..."

"Uh-oh. That doesn't look like a happy face."

"It was a very happy face until this afternoon. We spent some really great time with each other. It was almost like old times. We *fit* so well." After a long, deep sigh, I explained our exchange this afternoon.

Monica gave me a compassionate smile as the zen fountain trickled behind her. "What do you want Quinn to do?"

"I don't know. His words stung a lot. Like I'm not good enough to be around his son."

"Are you sure that's what he meant?"

"I don't know what he meant! He shut me down flat."

"Because you're leaving."

"Of course I'm leaving! I'm on vacation."

Monica laughed, but there was sympathy in it. "You sound confused."

"That might be the biggest understatement of the year. I can see myself with Quinn, and I think he feels the same."

"But he's not interested in a long-distance relationship."

I shrugged. "Who knows? I don't know! All I did was suggest dinner. We've never talked about what might happen after I go back to Tampa."

"Sounds like you two need to have a conversation."

"Yeah, I think you're right." I swept my gaze around the empty lobby. "I need to work up to that, though. Do you have more classes today?"

"No, this is the last one." Monica cocked her head. "Would you like to teach a class?"

That took me by surprise. "What do you mean?"

"I could pose as a beginner, and you could get some practice teaching. With only me in the class, you'd have less pressure. I've taught other yoga instructors."

"Oh, I couldn't impose like that!"

"I don't mind, Steph," Monica replied with a smile. "I enjoy fostering talent, and you've got plenty. I upped the difficulty of the class this afternoon and you handled it great."

I laughed, my face heating. "Not really. My handstands have been better. I think I'm going to hit the treadmill. Burn off some of this anxiety. But thanks for the offer."

"Anytime. Let me know if you change your mind."

I RAN FOR ALMOST AN HOUR, my mind still stuffed full of

Quinn. *What do I want?* The only way to find out was to talk to him.

I ate dinner at the pool bar, brushing off a guy who hit on me. I'd intentionally left my phone in the room. When I returned, there was a voice mail in addition to the texts from Quinn. It sent a guilty pang through me.

"Can we at least talk about this?" His voice was soft and pleading. "Please call me back, Steph."

I stared at the phone in my hands. How much heartache could have been prevented if I'd been more willing to talk after I broke up with him in college? I placed the call, and Quinn picked up immediately, out of breath. "Hey. Thanks for calling."

I couldn't resist a smile. "Did you run to the phone?"

"No, it's right here next to me. I'm lifting. I work out after Liam goes to sleep."

"That's a good time to do it."

"I didn't mean to speak harshly this afternoon. I'm sorry. We've been in this weird twilight zone since the other night... and it kind of lulled me into forgetting we live separate lives. I was upset and didn't put it well."

"I felt the same. I think we need to have a conversation, and I don't really want to do it over the phone. Can we get together tomorrow?"

His relief showed in his voice. "That would be great. Let's meet someplace private so we don't get interrupted."

"You know the place a lot better than me. What do you think?"

"There's nothing private about the dive shop or the marina. How about your room after I get back from the morning trip?"

I giggled. "Uh, that sounds like trouble, Quinn."

"I'll be a gentleman, don't worry."

"Maybe it's not you I'm worried about."

His soft laugh came through the phone. "I think we can both control ourselves... Steph, in college we parted under really rough circumstances. We need to talk about that. *I* need to talk about that."

That sounded slightly ominous, but he was right. "Okay. Come up to my room when you're back from the dive."

"Do you want to join the trip?"

"No, not this time."

"I can put you with Diego if you'd rather."

"It's not that. I booked a treatment at the spa for tomorrow morning. It will take several hours."

"Oh." He sounded disappointed, and my heart twisted at the gulf once again between us. Quinn took a long breath. "I'll see you shortly after noon, then."

Chapter Twenty

Quinn

THE FOLLOWING MORNING, Diego and I stayed aboard *Aqua Dreams*, changing over tanks while Sam and the group of divers waded ashore to spend the surface interval at a protected beach. Sam carried a backpack filled with soft drinks and snacks he set out on a driftwood log on the tiny strip of white sand beach.

I had been tense all morning, needing to put in a serious effort to remain upbeat with my divers. I was a mess of confused emotions over what to say to Steph. As I was sliding the tank band of a BCD over a tank, I trapped my thumb and pinched it. "Goddammit! Ouch." I shook my hand out, scowling at the offending equipment.

Diego peered at me. "What's eating you today? You've been growling all morning."

"Sorry. I was hoping it wasn't noticeable."

"Maybe not to the guests, but Sam and I have noticed. What's up?"

With a sigh, I flopped down onto the fiberglass side bench. "Woman trouble."

Diego flashed a grin. "Is there any other kind?"

I laughed, and it felt good to let some of the negative tension out. I needed to talk to someone about my dilemma, and Diego was the obvious choice. Especially since we had privacy at the moment. "Steph and I got together the other night. As in *together*."

Diego eyed me evenly. "I take it that was a mistake?"

"No. Yes. Hell, I don't know. It was fantastic. We talked for hours, and physically... wow. But she's met Liam, and everything is so damn complicated."

Diego sat next to me. "What do you mean?"

In as few words as possible, I explained our history. "When I saw Liam with her again yesterday, it brought reality full circle. She asked me to bring him and have dinner with her, and I shut her down cold." I explained why.

Diego furrowed his brow. "Is a casual dinner that big a deal? I admit this isn't my wheelhouse, but isn't it a good thing for Liam to see you with other people? I've had dinner with you two."

"I just don't want to confuse him. He's still reeling from his mother moving away. And Steph is leaving in a few days."

"Does Liam have any friends with divorced parents?"

"Yeah. Plenty—too many. That's the way it is these days."

Diego opened his mouth, then snapped it shut again.

I smiled. "Go on. What were you going to say?"

"Well, is it possible you're underestimating Liam? If you explain that Steph is someone you like and want to spend time with before she goes home, I don't see how that would confuse him. Especially if you told him she wanted to get to know him better. I think he might like that. Or does she not like him?"

"Not at all. They've fed Buster together. Twice." I rubbed my face with both hands. "God, I don't know what to do."

"Do you want to continue seeing her?"

"Not long distance. I can't leave Liam to fly off to Tampa on my days off."

"I thought he was leaving for the summer soon."

"Very soon."

Diego coiled a regulator in his hands. "So you've got several months to figure this out, right? Why not give it a shot and see where things stand at the end of the summer?"

I couldn't deny the appeal of that. After nine months of having Liam to myself, his absence was going to leave a massive chasm inside me. Liam was my priority, but it wasn't healthy for him to be my whole life. And it wasn't a case of wanting to fill the void with anyone. I'd been down that road before, and it didn't work for me.

I only wanted Steph.

"That's an idea," I said. "But a long-distance relationship wouldn't work when I've got Liam."

"You said that. Just as I said, cross that bridge when you get there." Diego paused, his warm brown eyes steady on me. "Can I say something and have you promise not to deck me?"

I twitched the corner of my mouth. "Depends on how much it pisses me off. I'll try to restrain myself, okay?"

"Are you sure all your hesitancy is about Liam? Or are you using him as an excuse not to get hurt again? Especially by Steph?"

My stomach dropped to the fiberglass deck of the boat.

"Honestly, that never occurred to me. But you could be right. That's something that's always upset me about how we ended. That Steph got her heart broken and I was the bad guy who got his new girlfriend pregnant. Like our breakup didn't rip me to pieces too. You might be right. Both of us would be risking a lot if we decided to give this another shot. That's why we're both so hesitant about it." I stared at a school of fish swimming in the shallows but saw Steph's face instead. "We're meeting today to talk things over after I get back to the dock. I'm not sure we'll decide anything, but we've both got some things to get off our chests."

Diego nodded and stood. The divers were returning to the boat. "I'll take care of getting the afternoon trip ready. You can take off as soon as we get back. Good luck, man. Whatever you decide."

Chapter Twenty-One

Steph

I CLOSED the door to my room, taking a moment to admire the dark-pink polish on my nails. I had spent the morning getting a massage, mani-pedi, and a body wrap that had left my skin soft as silk and practically glowing.

If only my mind were equally at ease.

Knowing the upcoming break would be Quinn's only chance to eat, I ordered two sandwiches from room service, which were delivered quickly. I set them on the small table, nervously fussing with the place settings.

Will he show up with that guarded, wary look in his eye? Do I dare to take a chance on him? He apologized for what he said, but how can we make this work?

The next knock came at 12:15, and my heart leaped into my mouth.

When I answered the door, Quinn stood there, tall and gorgeous, both hands in the pockets of his board shorts. He wore an expectant look as he stared at me with his head slightly ducked, like an adult version of a boy who had misbehaved and wasn't sure if he was about to get yelled at.

He was so adorable I couldn't help a smile as I waved him in, which broke up the dread circling inside me. "Hi there."

"Thanks for seeing me." Quinn swept into the room. He smelled faintly of salt water, and I did my best to resist his physical presence.

I moved toward the table. "I ordered lunch."

"That's great—I'm starved. Thanks."

We tiptoed verbally as we ate, discussing each other's mornings. When Quinn finished, he wiped his mouth with his napkin and tossed it on top of his empty plate. "Steph, I'm a mess. I don't know where we stand or where we're going. The only thing I know is that I'm sorry for how I spoke to you yesterday."

I nodded, sitting back in my chair. "Thanks. I'm not exactly clear on things, either. And you're right that we need to talk about this. Neither one of us thought meeting again was in the cards."

"No." Quinn held my gaze. "But I don't regret the other night."

"Neither do I. The question is, where do we go from here?"

He hesitated, fiddling with his fork on the plate. "This morning, I talked for quite a while with Diego. He's my best friend here, and he helped me realize one thing—that I'd like to keep seeing you. I'm just not sure how that's going to work."

I stood and moved to the sliding glass door to watch the sun sparkling on the ocean. My heart pounded at his admission—the same thing I was feeling. "Neither am I, and I want to see you too. I like it at the insurance company. It's a little on the mundane side, but I love being the person everyone counts on."

"You've always been the glue in whatever group you were in." Quinn pushed to his feet and stood behind me, grasping my shoulders with his hands. "Diego helped me get some perspective. With Liam being gone over the summer, I could come visit you in Tampa. You could come here. Maybe we can give this a shot."

Butterflies flitted around my abdomen. Hadn't I thought the same thing? "That might work. But what about when summer is over?"

"We'll have to cross that bridge when we get there." Quinn turned me to face him. His hands were light, yet firm on my shoulders. "I never stopped caring about you, Steph. Seeing you again was like a punch in the gut—that was how strongly you affected me. Now that I've got you back in my life, I don't want to let you go."

I wrapped my hands around his forearms, feeling the play of his muscles underneath. "I've always regretted how we ended. *That* we ended. At the time, I was so hurt, and getting past that seemed impossible. But looking back now, I can see how immature and judgmental I was. But those wounds are still there, Quinn. And you reopened them yesterday when you saw me and Liam together."

"Both of us have regrets. How will we know whether we can overcome them if we don't try?"

I broke away, moving to stand several feet away as my resolve built. "Here's the thing, Quinn. I'm not interested in being some dirty secret in your life that you don't want to tell anyone about—especially Liam. That's how you made me feel yesterday."

"I know. And I'd never be ashamed to show you off. You're the most amazing woman in any room you enter. But

I'm not sure you understand that Liam is a huge priority for me."

I whirled around, irritation rising like bile. "Of course I understand that! Do you think I'm some heartless bitch who wants to see your son hurt? You're exactly the kind of father I thought you'd be. I've only been around the two of you for a short period, but it's obvious in his face he worships you. But I refuse to get more involved with you if you won't let me into your life! Your whole life, Quinn."

"That's what I'm trying to do here!"

"By only seeing me when your son isn't around? What kind of message does that send to him?"

Quinn raked a hand through his hair. "He's not going to be around! That's part of the deal with Melody. He'll be gone for *three months*."

My breath caught, a black hollowness opening up inside. "Is that what this is about for you? You're going to miss Liam, so you're looking for someone to fill the hole he's leaving in your life?"

Parking his hands on both hips, Quinn faced me squarely. "No, dammit! My God, Steph. What I feel for you two is completely different. I love you both in totally different ways. Yes, he got me through the void that was left after I lost you. That's true—he was the only light during several really miserable years."

I caught that he'd said he still loved me but let it pass. It was probably a slip of the tongue, and I was too distraught for endearments. I wasn't the only one. Quinn was upset and getting more so by the minute.

He dripped frustrated tension, his jaw set tight. "Do you think our breakup only affected you? That you were the only one hurt? My life completely changed!"

I took a step toward him, meeting his anger with anger.

"Well, don't blame me for that. If you had kept your dick in your pants, things might be very different right now."

He scoffed. "I used a condom. It failed! And yeah, I admit Melody was a rebound relationship. I never wanted to marry her, and I'm a lot happier since we divorced."

"So what? Do you want me to applaud you or something?"

Quinn flinched, making me regret my words.

I took a deep breath and spoke more quietly. "I'm sorry. That was uncalled for. We both seem to have sharp tongues, don't we?"

Quinn let his hands fall to his sides, his chest heaving. The anger in his eyes disappeared, replaced with sheer pain. "Steph, you don't get it. We were in our final year of college—we'd been together for over two years."

He paused, then shook his head. "I was shopping for engagement rings. I was planning on asking you to marry me. That goddamn dive changed the entire course of our lives."

Goosebumps rippled down my arms and my mouth dropped open. That year we had talked about plans for after we graduated, kicking around the idea of getting an apartment together in Miami. But a marriage proposal was news to me.

Stunning news.

I took a step back, my knees suddenly weak. "I had no idea."

Quinn stared at me evenly, frustration still evident in his tense frame. "Now you do. I've always felt like you ended up the innocent victim in this and I was the callous villain. Like I didn't have a right to my own feelings. Or the right to grieve over what I lost too."

I stared at him, stunned at this revelation. And the truth of it. "I felt pretty self-righteous afterward. You're right—I played the wounded victim, unable to see my part in the whole debacle. I'm sorry about that. At least you got Liam out of it."

He briefly squeezed his eyes shut, his face a mask of pain. "Don't you see? That's one of the hardest things about this. I bitterly regret becoming involved with Melody. Because it cost me *you*. But Liam is the best thing that's ever happened to me. He made me want to be the best man I can. So how do I reconcile that?"

My heart was breaking anew. Both at the pain on Quinn's face and at what I had lost without even knowing. "I'm not sure. But I think it's going to involve having *both* of us in your life."

He straightened, eyeing me intently. "Do you think you can get past what happened between us? Or will Liam be a constant reminder, hurting you over and over? Will you think about me and Melody every time you see him?"

That made me angry again. "Why would I? He's a little boy, Quinn. He didn't have any say in this! I can look at him fine. The question is, can *you*?"

His face went blank. "What are you talking about?"

Regret turned to fury. My blood pressure ratcheted up. "Divorced parents get involved with people all the time! Several of my friends have been through it, and the kids learn to deal with it. After what you just said about us getting married, I'm wondering if *you're* the one having a hard time getting over our breakup. And you're using Liam as a shield."

I inhaled sharply as he stepped forward, his eyes blazing. Pure masculine fury and magnificent in every inch. "I am not hiding behind my son. God, Steph, what do you want from me?"

Glaring, I marched forward to close the distance between us. "I want to *matter* to you. I want to be a part of Liam's life. And yours."

Both of us were breathing hard. Angry heat poured off him in waves. "I already told you I'd do that. I love you both."

"You love me? Prove it."

Quinn grabbed my shoulders, yanking me toward him. He crushed his mouth to mine, a deep, wrenching moan escaping from his throat. I surrendered, melting against him, running both hands through his hair as I plunged my tongue into his mouth. He encircled his arms around me, squeezing my ass with both hands as he ground against me. Our kiss went on and on. Nothing else mattered except that he was in my arms. Not our past, not our future.

Only now.

Finally, I broke the kiss and leaned my cheek against his. "I love you too. I tried to stop, but I've never gotten over you. But God, this is hard."

Quinn left a trail of kisses across my cheek and pressed his lips to my ear. "We need to find out how to make this work. We're meant to be together. We've got to find a way."

I slid my arms around his waist, my anger spent. "So what now?"

With a sigh, he took a large, deliberate step back and looked at his watch. "For now, I have to get back to work. Will you dive tomorrow morning? I'm off the day after. So let's sleep on it tonight"—he smiled crookedly—"separately. And get together tomorrow. Maybe by then we'll have an idea."

I nodded, blood still thrumming through my veins. Along with confusion and regret. But I was able to see the sense in his words. "All right. I'll see you tomorrow morning."

Chapter Twenty-Two

Quinn

I STOOD APART from the other parents on the sideline, watching Liam complete running drills as practice wound down. After leaving Steph's room, my troubled mind had been occupied teaching an open water scuba class, but now it was free to wander. To ponder. I studied my son as Liam ran from sideline to sideline, bending over to touch the line before racing to the other side.

Am I making more of an issue over a relationship with Steph than it actually is?

I kept bouncing back and forth between yes and no. Which was no help at all.

After practice, we climbed into the golf cart. I turned the key and looked at Liam. "How about we stop by Pirate's Den and get dinner to go?"

"Yeah!" Liam's eyes lit up and I laughed. Pirate's Den was one of the tourist restaurants lining Buccaneer Marina. Not exactly a local hangout, but kids loved it. It was one of the tamer establishments that tolerated children, though I still would never take my son to the marina later, when the parties were in full swing.

When we pulled into our driveway, Liam clutched the white bag in both hands like a priceless treasure.

"Okay," I said, opening the front door. "Let's eat, then you need to take a shower or bath. Your choice." I spread out our hamburgers and fries, and Liam dove into his dinner. I watched him, amazed at his appetite. "You must be going through a growth spurt."

"I'm starving."

I grinned. "I can see that. And don't talk with your mouth full."

Liam's final soccer match of the season was in two days and had been weighing on my mind. The game was undeniable proof that time with my son was growing short. The Titans were making the journey from Miami to Sandpiper Cay to play the Sharks. I took a long breath and asked the question that had been on my mind all afternoon. "My friend Steph is leaving in a few days. How would you feel if I invited her to your soccer game?"

Liam swallowed, shrugging. "It's fine with me. Is she your girlfriend again?"

"We're still trying to figure that out. But when you two have fed Buster, she's enjoyed being around you."

"She's nice. Buster likes her—I can tell."

Liam stuffed another French fry in his mouth, and I relaxed. Liam had always been a quiet, perceptive child. He was very even-tempered, rarely throwing temper tantrums. The unruliest he'd ever been had been the previous autumn, when we had moved to Sandpiper Cay, and he knew he wasn't going to see his mother for months. But as he adjusted to his new reality, his natural personality soon reasserted itself, much to my relief.

I watched Liam closely but couldn't detect any signs he was upset at the thought of a potential woman in my life. The tight knot I'd been carrying around in my stomach all day finally relaxed.

"Steph is diving tomorrow morning," I said. "I'll ask her then."

"When can I start diving?" Liam was a water baby. He'd been swimming before he could walk and was at ease with a mask and snorkel.

"Pretty soon. You can take the bubblemaker class when you're eight. If you want, we can make that a goal for this fall after you come back from your mom's."

"Okay!" The eagerness on Liam's face warmed my heart. It might be a lonely summer without him, but now we had something special to look forward to in the fall.

Chapter Twenty-Three

Steph

THE WHITE WINE tasted crisp and cold as I sat on my balcony, watching the sun creep closer to the western horizon. I brushed my tongue over my bottom lip, closing my eyes as the feel—and the taste—of Quinn washed over me. We'd had plenty of conversation that afternoon, not to mention heated kisses, but I was as confused and muddled as ever.

And shocked.

He was going to ask me to marry him! What might have been?

Shaking my head, I took another sip. I had gotten through to him that being a part of Liam's life—not just Quinn's—was important to me. But Quinn had given me plenty to think about in return.

My phone rang on the table next to me, Jana's name lighting up the screen. I set down my glass and answered with a grin. "You know, the whole point of a vacation is to get away from work."

An indignant gasp sounded through the phone. "How dare you! You assume I'm calling because I've got a work problem? Maybe I only want an update on Mr. Right Again?"

"So you don't have a work problem?"

"Well..."

I burst into laughter. "I know. I need to do something about my suspicious mind."

"It's not a huge problem. You can probably solve it in two seconds."

"Lay it on me then."

"My shared drive disappeared."

With a sigh, I grabbed my wine and entered the air-conditioned room, opening my laptop on the desk. "Give me a second to log in. How did the meeting with Roger go?"

"Great! I had everything he asked for. Well, except he wanted to know exactly when you'd be back. And I dropped all the file folders as I entered the boardroom."

Laughing, I needed only minutes to instruct Jana on how to find the correct drive, which was exactly where it always was. If it were anyone but Jana on the line, I would be suspicious they made up the lost drive story and had ulterior motives. But the shared drive problem was pure Jana.

"Okay, the universe is safe once again," Jana said breathlessly. "Tell me all about your hot, tropical nights with Quinn."

"There haven't been any more."

"What? Your vacation is almost done! Oh... is your relationship over already?"

"No, it's definitely not over between us. In fact, we just talked about it, and both of us want to continue seeing each other."

"That's great news, isn't it?"

"It's complicated news. He can't hop on a plane and come see me."

At least until Liam goes to Melody's.

"Steph McIntyre, I've known you for six years. I've never seen you so interested in a guy you'd consider a long-distance relationship."

"That's because Quinn isn't just another guy."

"Then hop on a plane and go see him."

I took a sip of wine, considering the idea. "I could do that. In fact, I'll probably have to do a lot of that."

"You don't sound very enthusiastic. Is it because you're afraid he'll rip your heart out again and stomp on it some more?"

Quinn's anguished face as he told me about shopping for an engagement ring flashed into my mind, and I closed my eyes. That information, and my reaction, was still too fresh and raw to bring up. "I think we've moved past that now. I wasn't the only one who got hurt, and I've owned up to my part in our breakup. But we aren't two kids about to graduate from college anymore. We have to figure out how to make this work in our current lives."

"Any chance he'd move to Tampa? I'm sure there are shops who need dive instructors."

"None. He wants to set down roots and provide stability for Liam."

Jana sighed dreamily. "I can't believe I'm saying this, and don't take it the wrong way. But is there any chance of you moving to Sandpiper Cay?"

That idea nearly stopped my heart. I was settled in my life in Tampa. Settled... that described my life perfectly.

Have I settled too much?

Monica's offer of a mock yoga class fluttered through my

head, but I pushed it away, heart pounding. "I have a good-paying, steady job. Maybe my life isn't the most exciting in the world, but I'm happy."

"Suit yourself. I'd hate to lose you and you know it. But if things work out with Quinn, eventually someone will have to move, right?"

"We were talking today about seeing how things go this summer, then make a decision in the fall on whether to continue."

"Gawd! That sounds as romantic as a root canal."

I burst into laughter. "Yeah, you're right."

"Come on! It's Sandpiper Cay. One of you needs to dodge limbo dancers and leap over a fallen palm tree to reach the other as they're leaving."

"We'll see what we can come up with," I said dryly.

"When do you see him again?"

"Tomorrow morning. I'm going diving for the final time this trip. Then I've got an unscheduled day before it's back to Tampa."

"And me! Don't forget about me!"

"How could I?" I missed Jana's earnest, funny face and mop of curly hair.

"Steph?"

"Still here, babe."

"What's going on between you and Quinn... it sounds like something that doesn't come around very often. Or ever. I know you two have a lot to work out, but don't throw this relationship away because of what happened before."

"Thanks. I only realize now how much Quinn's life was devastated. If there's one thing we've figured out, it's that we've missed each other, and we still love each other."

But can you let me into your life fully, Quinn?

"I have to admit I'll be dying of curiosity to find out

what happens," Jana said. "Call me when you get home. Or even a text so I know you made it home safe."

"I'll do that." As I ended the call, I couldn't help but agree with Jana.

I'm dying of curiosity to find out what happens too.

Chapter Twenty-Four

Steph

I SHINED my dive light on the sea fan, entranced when the drab, dark fronds transformed into an electric orange under direct light. Glancing at my dive computer, a surge of pride ran through me. I was at one hundred feet, moving with confidence and completely in control. From the front of the group, Quinn turned around and flashed an okay signal at me, raising his brows.

Smiling around my regulator, I firmly nodded. He nodded back, his eyes softening. This site wasn't the one where I'd panicked and nearly drowned eight years ago, but it was a similar depth.

And a major milestone for me.

I turned my light toward another fan. On a dive as deep as this, the colors of the spectrum were filtered out except for blue, causing the reef to look dull and monochromatic without additional illumination. The only other time I had dived deep enough to experience the phenomenon, I'd been too terrified to notice. When the beam of my light shined on the second fan, its color exploded into brilliant purple. It was an exhilarating sight—one I never would have experienced without taking the risk of diving again.

The current here was minimal, barely enough to make the tips of the soft corals bend in the direction of the flow of water. I had made tremendous strides over my vacation, now confident at the depth that had nearly ended me.

And Quinn was a large part of why I had overcome my fear.

He was at the front of the group, showing the diver next to him something he'd found. The man gave him an okay signal and moved off. Quinn scanned the remaining divers until his eyes met mine. I couldn't define exactly how his gaze changed, but the look he was sending my way was meant for me alone. A tingle ran through my body as I kicked forward, smiling at him.

He beckoned me before holding his hand out. Enclosing mine within, he drew me to his side, and a slow, delicious roll ran through my body at the touch. Steadying me, Quinn used his free hand to point his light to something on a coral head. At first, I couldn't see the creature. Then its features became distinguishable from its surroundings, and I laughed.

The frogfish was about four inches long and sat perched at the edge of a piece of coral. A slightly brighter yellow than the hard coral it sat on, the ambush predator sat ready for any unwary fish or crustaceans that might swim by. Lumpy, misshapen, and with a prominent, down-turned mouth that gave it a perpetual frown, frogfish were always a treasure for divers. Their ability to camouflage made them hard to spot, and I gave Quinn's hand a solid squeeze, acknowledging his skill in finding the animal. He squeezed back before letting go, and I inhaled a lungful of air, rising up so I could make way for the next diver in line.

When I had boarded that morning, neither Quinn nor I acknowledged our romantic relationship. He had been busy preparing the group for the morning's dive and I didn't want special treatment. Well, not too much special treatment anyway. The small amount he was showing me was *very* nice, the way his thumb brushed my hand when he steadied me, and the frequent checks to confirm I was comfortable.

On the boat before submerging, he'd made sure I was okay with a deep dive. Though I didn't have my advanced certification, being near Quinn filled me with confidence. Eager to fully overcome my bad experience, I agreed to the dive enthusiastically.

Now, as Quinn finished showing the frogfish to the final diver, I was very glad I had.

After returning to the boat, I was slightly chilled after being submerged for an hour. Wanting more sun, I moved to the stern section and leaned on a table that held dive cameras.

Quinn finished the last tank and joined me, his short, dark hair still wet. He brushed my elbow, sending a jolt through my body. "You did great on that deep dive. You should be proud."

"I am." I could hardly keep the smile off my face. "And that frogfish was a wonderful find. You really have eagle eyes."

Quinn smiled and shook his head, but I could see the pride in his eyes. "It's usually there somewhere. It moved to that tan part of the reef, which made it easier to spot this time. I'm glad you got to see it."

I met his pale blue eyes and held them. "Me too. Thank you. You've made a real difference helping me dive again."

His eyes crinkled as he smiled. "So have you. And you're not running off the boat anymore to get away from me, which is a plus."

I laughed, enjoying our easy banter and how much we'd grown. "Coming back was a good idea."

He turned to watch the long white wake following the boat. "Do you have plans tomorrow?"

A nervous tremor ran through my abdomen. I'd purposely kept my day open. "Nothing yet. I was hoping we might spend some of it together."

"Me too." He took a deep breath in through his nose, then exhaled it. "Liam has a soccer game tomorrow morning at ten. It's here at the local field. Would you like to come with me to watch?"

I didn't think my smile could get bigger, but it did. "I'd love to. Thank you, Quinn." I brushed my hand over his arm, acknowledging his effort to include me.

"Mom and Dad will probably be there too. Is that okay?"

"Of course. I'd enjoy talking to them again." I paused, needing to say more. "This really means a lot to me, and I know this decision wasn't easy for you. Thank you."

He turned to me, his eyes serious. "I want you in my life, Steph. Let's work on this."

"I feel the same way."

Quinn broke into a crooked smile, lightening the mood. "You know a lot more about soccer than I do, though I've learned the longer Liam has played. Maybe you can give me some pointers."

I laughed. "I haven't played since college. Plus, something tells me you probably read a book or spent hours watching YouTube, so you'd know all about it for him."

Quinn's grin nearly split his face. "Only one book, but there were a lot of videos. And I'm sure you can still run rings around me."

"Where's the field?"

"Behind the school."

I cocked my head, picturing a large area full of brush and stunted trees. "The vacant lot?"

"Not so vacant anymore. They turned it into a general-purpose field several years ago. That made it easier when I formed our soccer team last fall—we already had a place to play."

"I'll be there. What's the rest of your day like today?"

"I'm guiding the afternoon trip, then leading a night dive. You want to come?"

I wrinkled my nose. "I'll pass. I'm not upsetting the apple cart when diving's going so well for me. I'll stick to daytime for now." I winked slowly at him. "Night is for other things."

My heart broke into a gallop as his smile became wolfish. "I couldn't agree more. Enjoy your afternoon and evening. I miss you already." With a soft brush of his hand over mine, he moved to stand next to Captain Sam.

AFTER A LAZY LUNCH and some pool time, I attended a late-afternoon yoga class. This one had a few more students, though was still less busy than I expected for such a beautiful facility. Monica strolled around as she taught, correcting people's postures and encouraging one struggling, but determined man. During the class, I watched the people around me, picking up on corrections I'd make if I were teaching.

As usual, I waited until the other guests had filed out before approaching Monica at the counter.

"You've got to be coming to the end of your trip!" the instructor said.

I laughed ruefully. "I am. Tomorrow's my last full day, then I'm scheduled for the twelve thirty p.m. ferry and a flight to Tampa on Sunday."

Monica leaned casually against the rose-colored glass counter. "We'll have to exchange email addresses. I've enjoyed getting to know you."

"Me too. You've been a great sounding board, and I've needed that. Thank you."

"Of course. Are you and Quinn getting along well?"

"Yes. Things are still unsettled, but he asked me to attend Liam's soccer game tomorrow morning. That was a huge step forward."

"Progress! You two have come a long way. He hurt you badly, and you wanted him to make some gesture that he was different now."

My smile faded, and I grew pensive. Monica's words had touched a part of my heart that had been troubled since the conversation with Quinn in my room.

Monica arched a brow. "What's that expression about?"

"Oh... what you just said. That he hurt me badly. The thing is, I learned yesterday I hurt him as much." Monica leaned forward over the counter, and her eyes grew so sympathetic, I found myself once again wanting to open up to her. "He told me that he'd been shopping for engagement rings right before we broke up. I had no idea."

"Wow. He tried to work it out afterward, didn't he?"

My voice grew soft, regret filling me. "Yeah. I wouldn't

talk to him. And Melody was right there, waiting to pick up the pieces. By the time I realized my mistake, it was too late."

"And now he's reached out with the gesture you were looking for. Maybe he's wanting you to do the same?"

I pondered Monica's question. How had I met Quinn halfway? Answer—I hadn't. "You're right. Asking me to Liam's game was a huge step for Quinn. I need to give a little too." Jana's words about visiting Sandpiper Cay more often entered my head.

But I had a better idea. Certainty flooded through me, grounding me solidly.

I held Monica's gaze, a smile spreading across my face. "Are you still willing to let me do a mock yoga class with you as my victim?"

Monica laughed as she straightened. "Absolutely! This was my final class of the day. I've got all evening if you want."

"I don't think we'll need that long. Hopefully, after one class, you'll be able to tell me if I have any future as a yoga instructor."

Monica beckoned as she headed back toward the studio. "Well, let's get started, then."

Chapter Twenty-Five

Quinn

I RINSED salt water off a dive mask and hung it on a peg in the drying rack. Despite my best efforts, my mind kept drifting back to Steph and the conversation we'd had after the morning dive trip. I was still a mess of confused emotions. We'd cleared the air a little, and I wanted to keep seeing her, but the logistics were daunting.

My phone buzzed in my pocket, and I pulled it out. Melody's name flashed on the screen, and I huffed a sigh. I had no desire to chat with my ex-wife, but I knew it was probably about Liam's upcoming visit, so I swiped to answer.

"Hey," I said, trying to keep my voice neutral.

"Hi, Quinn." Melody's voice was light and cheerful. She'd made more of an effort lately to be pleasant.

"What's up?" I asked, keeping my tone neutral.

"Just wanted to confirm everything's still on for next Saturday. Craig and I are really looking forward to seeing Liam. We've got a whole bunch of fun activities planned."

My jaw clenched at the mention of Craig, Melody's new boyfriend. It wasn't jealousy—I was long past that stage—but I still couldn't help a surge of protectiveness over my son.

"Is Liam excited about coming? He hasn't mentioned it much on our calls."

I hesitated, my gut tightening. Liam had been pretty quiet about the upcoming visit, and I knew his feelings were mixed. After finally settling in here, he wasn't altogether thrilled about leaving for several months.

"Yeah, he's looking forward to it," I said, trying to sound convincing. I didn't want to create any more tension between Melody and Liam. She was his mother, and I wanted them to have a good relationship, even if it was long-distance.

"That's good to hear," Melody replied. There was a slight pause, and then she asked, "So how are *you* doing, Quinn?"

The question caught me off guard. It was rare for Melody to ask about anything other than Liam. "Fine," I said shortly. "The dive shop has been busy, and Liam's soccer is keeping me busy."

Another pause, then Melody said, her voice dropping a notch, "Are you seeing anyone?"

I froze, my grip tightening on the phone. I hadn't expected that question.

Steph's face flashed into my mind, her hazel eyes sparkling with laughter. A surge of desire, so potent it almost hurt, ran through me. I had to take a deep breath to steady myself.

"Yeah." The word came out rougher than I intended. I paused to clear my throat, then surprised myself at what came out of my mouth. "I've met someone, but it's really new. We're just... seeing where things go."

I hadn't expected to say anything about a relationship to Melody. But there it was, out in the open.

"Oh?" Her voice sharpened. "Anyone I know?"

"Melody..."

"Come on! What's her name?"

Irritation flared inside me, now mixed with a fierce protectiveness toward Steph. I didn't want to talk about her with Melody. "None of your business," I snapped.

Instead of getting defensive like I'd expected, Melody surprised me by letting out a soft sigh. "Okay, Quinn. I get it. And honestly, I think it's a good thing you're seeing someone. You've been alone since we broke up, and just because things didn't work out between us doesn't mean you should never date again."

My anger deflated, replaced by a cautious relief. This wasn't the Melody I was used to. The Melody who had always been insecure and quick to take offense.

"I appreciate that," I said, my voice softening a little.

"I trust you to choose someone who'll be a good influence on Liam," she continued. "I know you'll always put him first."

I couldn't help a sly smile. Melody had always been jealous of Steph, even after we were married. Jealous of my memories of her. I wondered how Melody would feel if she knew exactly who I was seeing. Except I wasn't exactly seeing Steph, was I?

God this was complicated. "You're right. I will."

"Okay, then," Melody said. "I'll let you get back to work. Just let me know those flight details when you have them."

"Will do. Talk to you later." I ended the call and rubbed

a hand over my face, my mind whirling. Melody's unexpected maturity had thrown me for a loop. Maybe we were finally reaching a point where we could be civil, even friendly, for Liam's sake.

Pushing thoughts of Melody aside, I prepared equipment for the night dive. But underneath the relief of a cordial conversation with my ex-wife, a knot of anxiety tightened in my gut. I wanted Steph in my life. I *needed* her. But how could I make it work, knowing Liam was leaving soon and she was hundreds of miles away?

Focus on your damn job, man!

I grabbed a BCD in each hand and headed toward the boat. At least staying busy would keep Steph off my mind for a few hours.

Maybe.

Weariness seeped into my bones as I opened the front door of my parents' house. My father had a baseball game on the TV at low volume, and Liam was sound asleep on the couch. I exchanged a nod with Dad.

"Your mother is in the kitchen," he said softly, jerking his head across the room.

I passed through the wide entryway to where my mother sat at the table, working on a crossword puzzle. A delicious, spicy aroma permeated the area. "Sorry I'm so late," I said. A glance at the wall clock told me it was worse than I'd thought—getting close to 9:00 p.m. "The night dive went later than I thought it would."

"Oh, stop!" Mom rose and removed a stainless steel bowl from the refrigerator. She crossed to a covered crock-pot on the counter—the source of the amazing aroma making my stomach growl loudly. "Your night dives always end around this time. Last I saw, Liam was nodding off on the couch with your father."

"It's more than nodding off. He's out cold."

Mom opened two hamburger buns and piled a generous serving of pulled pork on each, topping them with coleslaw from the bowl. Then she crossed to the table, pulled out a chair, and patted the wooden back. "Sit. Eat. I know you're hungry."

I pressed a kiss on top of my mother's head as I pulled out the chair. "I'm starving. Thanks, Mom." After sitting, I took an enormous bite, eating one third of the sandwich, then closed my eyes and groaned.

Mom laughed as she took a seat adjacent to me. "You need to take better care of yourself. Did you even eat lunch?"

"Not much. I wolfed down a protein bar and soda between dives."

Unlike the previous day, when Steph had ordered room service to ensure I ate. I felt good about what we'd accomplished. A lot was still up in the air, but we both wanted to keep seeing each other. And I'd finally voiced my simmering resentments, clearing the air enough to reach out further to her.

"What time is Liam's game tomorrow? He wasn't sure."

"Ten." I paused in my annihilation of dinner, dabbing my mouth with a napkin. I met Mom's eyes. "You should probably know—I invited Steph. She'll be there with me."

My mother's eyes opened wide, and she grasped my forearm to squeeze tightly. "I'm so glad! I'd love to have a chance to talk to her again."

"Take it easy, Mom. Don't give her the third degree, okay?"

As I finished the second sandwich, gentle laughter

tumbled out of her mouth. "Don't worry. I won't. Are you two back together?"

"We're getting there. Inviting her tomorrow was a pretty big deal for me."

"I know," she said softly. "I've been worried about you. Melody was never my favorite person, but I'm still sorry your marriage didn't work out. I've been surprised that you're not... happier since you returned home."

I sat back in my chair, tossing my napkin on the empty plate in front of me. "I've been focused on Liam's happiness, not mine."

Mom patted my arm firmly. "He *is* happy, Quinn. His attitude is light years from where it was when you moved here. He's a well-adjusted, secure boy who knows his father would do anything for him."

"That's true. And you and Dad have been indispensable."

"Thank you. But my point is, it's time for you to stop worrying about Liam so much and start worrying about your own life. I'm really happy you and Steph are talking again."

I stood and drew my mother into an embrace. "Thanks. I am too. Tomorrow feels like the opening move. As to what happens next? Only time will tell."

For the moment, I'd take things with Steph one step at a time. I'd reached out and she accepted the gesture. The ball was in her court now. Maybe she could get time off during the summer for another visit? If we were going to work out as a couple, she would have to make a serious effort to visit Sandpiper Cay frequently.

That's a problem for the future.

Returning to the living room, I whispered good night to my father before gathering Liam up in my arms. The boy hardly stirred, just settled with his head against my shoulder. We walked into the warm night, and the Milky Way streaked above us. I made a mental note to remember this feeling—of relishing the time I had with my son, yet with something new to look forward to. I'd been dreading the rapidly approaching summer all year. But maybe the months weren't to be feared after all.

Tomorrow would tell...

Chapter Twenty-Six

Steph

CHEERING, followed by a collective moan, filled the morning air as Liam kicked the ball and the Titan goalie deflected it out of bounds. I applauded him, hardly able to believe I was there. And how happy I was—at what I had hopefully set in motion.

But there had been no time, or privacy, to discuss that. I'd find a way to get Quinn alone later. He sat to my left, his knee occasionally brushing mine. I'd met him and Liam at the field after walking from the Coral Queen. The morning was soft and welcoming, and I didn't want Quinn to disturb his and Liam's normal game-day routine on my account. Bruce and Brenda arrived shortly before the match started. Both had worn giant smiles at seeing me, and I forestalled any awkwardness by greeting each of them with a hug. Brenda set up her chair on my right, with Bruce on her other side.

Liam played midfield during the first half and now was at forward. I was impressed with his ball-handling skills, especially his kick on goal. With a team of seven- and eight-year-olds, my expectations had been rather low, but they moved the ball down the field efficiently. Only a few kids were more interested in watching butterflies, but they brought their own entertainment.

With a burst of speed, Liam kicked the ball smartly, but a defender intercepted and moved it around him, booting it down the field in the opposite direction.

"Dang!" I said, pounding my fists on my thighs.

Brenda grinned at me. "I'm sure you're following this much better than I am. Do you still play soccer?"

A girl kicked the ball out of bounds, and I turned to Brenda as the teams reset. "No, not since college. And I wasn't any great shakes there, either. But it was fun." I turned to Quinn and swept an arm across the expanse before us. "What a great field, and an actual league! We sure didn't have anything like this when we were kids."

Brenda laughed. "We didn't have the league even a year ago. Quinn started it when he moved here."

Quinn shrugged but couldn't resist lifting one side of his mouth. "I wanted to make sure Liam had something important to ground him here. He's been playing soccer since he was three."

The look in Quinn's eyes made my heart feel too full for my chest, like there wasn't enough room for it. "He's a lucky boy. I'm sure forming a league on an island was no small feat."

Quinn grinned. I loved seeing how relaxed he was, a smile lighting his face. "Finding a coach was the tough part, but a personal trainer at Sandpiper Pump coached junior high soccer previously. I shamelessly recruited him with visions of grandeur. By the time he realized the truth, it was too late, and he was committed."

"I imagine he knew what he was in for," I said with a laugh. "Visions of grandeur and kids' soccer don't exactly go together."

"How are your parents?" Brenda asked me. "We still exchange Christmas cards."

Sandpiper Cay was a small community. Though resort workers came and went, those who had put down roots were tight-knit. "They're doing very well. Both have taken to golf like they were born to it. How's the fishing business?"

On Brenda's other side, Bruce leaned forward to meet my eyes. "I sold the business two years ago and stayed on as a captain. I've cut back my hours—it's nice to have a paycheck but not the worries of running the business."

"I can understand that." I was sure Quinn was relieved too that his parents had been able to divest the enterprise successfully. He'd never been interested in fishing, and the family business had been a source of conflict during our college years.

College years... and now here I am again back on Sandpiper Cay. Enjoying myself, no less.

Which naturally led to thoughts of what the future might bring. My yoga session with Monica acting as a newbie had gone well. With only the instructor there, my nerves had been non-existent. I'd led Monica through a standard beginner Vinyasa class. Several times, Monica had performed poses incorrectly and I had successfully redirected her.

After I moved Monica's foot position for extended side angle pose, she straightened with a nod. "Great job. You've got an eye for how to reposition people, which is important. And I liked the flow of poses during your class. I think you'll be a great yoga instructor."

I beamed under the praise. "Thank you! That's encouraging to hear."

"You want me to email you the job application?"

I nodded and we exchanged email addresses, which we were planning on doing anyway. I wanted to hear all about Bali.

Monica jotted a note on a pad near the register. "I'll make sure you get an interview before you leave. Fill out the application ASAP, then look for the reply."

"Believe me, I'll be looking for it!"

Monica shook her head as she studied me. "The change in you is pretty remarkable compared to when you first arrived. Quinn has been good for you."

"Thanks. We've been good for each other. I've been floundering for a while now—kind of paralyzed. Coming here and seeing him broke me out of my trance."

"I admire Quinn," Monica said. "He's a single dad trying to do everything himself. I'm sure he'd love to have someone special around."

The very thought of that made me excited. "That's what I'm hoping too."

It was rather amazing how less than two weeks of vacation had completely changed my perspective. My hardworking, go-to persona of the insurance company now looked like a woman desperately hiding from life.

My blinders were off permanently.

Now, I watched Liam race down the field as he focused on the midfielder handling the ball. The constant action on the field helped me fight the urge to check my email on my phone.

The job application had been in my inbox when I woke up that morning. I had stared at it as I drank a cup of coffee, fingers drumming rhythmically on the trackpad of my laptop. When my mug was empty, I set it on the desk with a firm thump and filled out the application. Now I was waiting to find out when my interview was. But there was no doubt I was cutting it close—I was scheduled on the 12:30 ferry tomorrow afternoon.

Anticipation sent shivers down my arms at the thought of telling Quinn what I'd done. He'd reached out to me, out of his comfort zone. Now it was my turn to return the gesture. But we needed to be alone. A soccer game with his parents on my other side was anything but private. Quinn had invited me for ice cream with himself and Liam after the match. Maybe I'd get some alone time then.

The midfielder passed the ball to Liam, who deftly kicked it past the player in front of him. One last defender and the goalkeeper were the only players between him and the goal.

"Come on, Liam!" I shouted as we all stood.

The boy made a sharp kick, slanting the ball past as the goalie dove for it. The net swished as it caught the ball and all four of us burst into applause.

Quinn cupped his hands around his mouth and shouted, "That's how you do it!"

Liam turned from his celebration with teammates and gave his father a thumbs-up.

Quinn turned his smile to me. My heart hammered against my chest at his handsome, blissful face. And at how happy I was.

I could get used to this.

I took another heavenly spoonful of coconut ice cream as I watched a gigantic snorkeling catamaran motor through the canal on its way to the open ocean. Quinn, Liam, and I were at Tropical Creamery, located at Buccaneer Marina. Quinn ate pecan ripple and Liam was nearly done with his chocolate chip. The ice cream parlor was on the very edge of the marina, trying its best to accommodate both the fun-seeking tourists and locals who brought their kids for a treat.

"You've got great ball-handling skills," I said to Liam.

"Thanks. I've worked hard this season."

"Your dad and I didn't have anything this nice when we grew up here," I said. "I didn't start playing soccer until we went to college at Miami."

Liam's eyes grew huge. "You played soccer for the Miami Hurricanes?"

I shook my head and grinned. "Hardly. Just a rec league, but I really enjoyed it."

"Did you get to play in a big stadium?"

I smiled, remembering the awe I'd felt looking at the ring of empty seats surrounding me. "We did once, when we made the finals in a tournament. That was pretty cool."

Liam gave an exaggerated nod, his eyes still enlarged. "I bet it was. What position did you play?"

"Mostly midfielder. I was hardly pro material."

"Don't let Steph's modesty fool you," Quinn piped in. "She was really good. I used to go to her matches and cheer when everyone else did. Other than scoring goals, I had no idea what a good play was."

Liam's eyes darted between the two of us, and I had the feeling he didn't miss much. His gaze settled on me. "You don't play anymore?"

"No. Until today, I haven't been on a soccer field since college. So thank you, Liam."

"Welcome." He grinned and took another giant bite from his waffle cone, nearly to the bottom.

"I also like that your league is both boys and girls." When I had been growing up, activities for girls had been few and far between. I was glad to see that changing on Sandpiper Cay.

Liam shrugged. "Girls are okay. Doesn't make a difference to me." He stuffed the last bite in his mouth, chewed a couple of times, then swallowed and held up both hands. "There! I'm all done. Can I play with Grayson now?"

"Go for it," Quinn said. Soon after their arrival, Liam's friend Grayson and his family had shown up, and now the boys were more interested in playing on the ice cream shop's playground than eating.

I laughed as he tore away, joining Grayson on the jungle gym. Ice cream dripped down the side of my cone. "Liam can have the playground. I'm loving this ice cream."

My hand froze midway to my mouth as Quinn pressed the length of his thigh against mine. "I'm loving the privacy we have all of a sudden."

Meeting Quinn's gaze, I took a long lick of ice cream, wiping the errant line from the cone. His eyes devoured every movement.

"So am I," I murmured and reluctantly tore my gaze away.

The two boys took off toward Grayson's parents, standing side by side before them. I smiled as they gesticulated before the two adults. "I can see why he's going to have a hard time leaving for the summer. He seems to have settled in really well here."

"He has. I'm proud of him."

I nodded at Grayson. "And he has something to look forward to when he returns."

"Hopefully lots of things."

Liam jumped up and down before spinning on his heel

and taking off toward us at top speed. He skidded to a stop in front of his father, eyes wide with expectation. "Grayson's parents said I could sleep over tonight, since it's our last weekend before I take off. Can I? Can I?"

Quinn laughed, sitting back in his chair. "Okay! Take it easy, buddy. We'll go home so you can shower, change, and pack an overnight bag."

Liam's expression fell. "I don't need to. Can't I go straight to Grayson's? That will save you having to drive me over."

I grinned at his use of logic, at all of seven years old.

"No," Quinn said firmly. "You're still sweaty from the game. Shower first. Go on and play now."

"All right." With a laugh, Liam returned to the playground and Grayson.

Quinn unfolded his long legs and rose from the table too. "I'd better talk to Grayson's folks and make sure this is okay."

I watched him as he ambled over. Though not surprised he was a good father, it was heartwarming to watch him in action. I'd always pictured myself having children, but that had never come to pass. I'd never found a man I wanted to be that close to.

Quinn was soon back and sat down again. "They're happy to have him as soon as I get him packed and ready." He met my gaze evenly. "Why don't you come with? You can keep me company in the golf cart after we drop him off." His eyes sparkled, saying loud and clear the golf cart wasn't the company he had in mind.

I laughed softly. "Deal. That will give me a chance to say goodbye to Liam too. You're really great at this father thing. You never wanted more than one child?"

Quinn paused, his eyes meeting mine before dropping

to his ice cream again. "Not with Melody. I tried to make the marriage work. And she did too. But I didn't want to bring another child into that environment, and Melody wasn't interested in more kids anyway."

My heart twisted at his simple, honest admission. "I'm sorry, Quinn."

His eyes whipped up. "What for?"

"For the pain you've been through. And for the fact that I never knew it. I'd always pictured you happy in your new life, without me."

"I was never happy without you. Just... living."

Our eyes locked together, the moment lengthening. Quinn leaned forward and swept his lips over mine, a soft kiss for a public place. When he spoke, his face was an inch from mine. "With Liam sleeping over at Grayson's, we have until tomorrow morning. Let's get out of here. Liam will have plenty of time with his friend tonight, but the clock is ticking for you and me."

A slow smile crept across my face. Plenty of privacy for the news I wanted to give him! "Your place or mine?"

"Mine. It's roomier. And I don't want you to feel like we have to hide away in a hotel room."

I traced my fingers over the rough skin on the back of his hand. "I don't feel like your dirty little secret."

"Good. You shouldn't. You aren't."

"Neither are you." I rose and held out my hand to him. "Let's go."

Chapter Twenty-Seven

Quinn

THE PAVEMENT WAS smooth under the golf cart's tires as I drove along picturesque Lakeshore Boulevard. To the sides, ornate lampposts arched overhead, with wrought-iron benches perched beneath carefully planted palm trees. In the distance, a large gate crossed the road, preventing access to the ritzy mansions in the distance. Private docks extended into the ocean, many with thatched palapas at the end and mammoth yachts tied alongside.

Steph blew a long, low whistle. "Boy, this has changed in the last eight years."

I turned the golf cart around at the gate, heading back toward Portsmouth. "Yeah, some real A-list celebrities and rich folks have homes here. And more are available to rent—for a price, of course."

After dropping Liam off at Grayson's, Steph had wanted a tour of Portsmouth. I was still on a high from the whole morning and how normal it had been. Steph and me, along with my parents, watching a kids' soccer match. I hadn't worried about Steph interacting with my parents, but it had warmed me how much they had enjoyed being around each other.

And Steph had only cemented my feelings when she had said goodbye to Liam as he left the golf cart at Grayson's. Low-key, and without drama, she'd simply said, "Thanks for letting me come to your soccer game and feed Buster. I'm glad I got to meet you, Liam."

He'd looked back at her and smiled. "Me too. If you come around again, maybe we can kick the ball around some."

"One hundred percent. I look forward to it."

Thereby telling Liam she *would* be around again and giving him a reason to look forward to the occasion. I reached over and took her hand as we traveled down Main Street.

As we passed a colorful one-story building boasting a purple and pink exterior, Steph broke into laughter. "I can't believe it! Emerson's Emporium is still around?"

The eclectic little-bit-of-everything store had been a mainstay for as long as I could remember. "Some things never go out of style, I guess. You want to stop and look around?"

She squeezed my hand. "No, keep going. I've got less than twenty-four hours left before I have to be on the ferry. I want to make them count."

I forced a smile to my face, but my heart plummeted. I didn't want to think about that yet. I turned onto my street. "We'll make it count. Don't worry."

After entering my house, we made straight for the back porch. I grabbed two beers from the fridge as I passed. We sat at the patio table and clinked our bottles together. "To a successful vacation," I said. "You made remarkable progress diving this week, Steph. I mean it. I'm really proud of you."

"Thanks. So am I. It's hard to believe now how close I came to not diving when I saw you." Her eyes were serious when they met mine. "Thanks for being persistent. You didn't give up."

"That last dive we did was one of the biggest regrets of my life. When I saw my chance at redemption, I wasn't going to let it go."

Steph shook her head. "I was a stupid kid about that. I overreacted and was judgmental. And by the time I realized my mistake, I'd already lost you."

I sat back in my chair with a long sigh. "When Melody told me she was pregnant, I felt like my life was over, even as we made plans to get married. Then two days later, you said you wanted to get back together, which only cemented my mood. But there was no way I could turn my back on them."

Steph flashed me a sad smile. "Of course not. Even then, I realized you wanted to do the right thing. A part of me always wondered if Melody got pregnant on purpose to trap you, or if you really loved her."

"No, the birth control just failed." I paused, not really wanting to talk about my ex-wife, but recognizing now was the time to fully deal with our past if we were to move beyond it. "But I never loved her. Never. I was thinking about breaking up with her when she told me she was pregnant. I thought we could learn to love each other eventually, but that never happened."

"For both of you?"

I hesitated, then shrugged uncomfortably. "On my end, mostly, though she was really unhappy by the end too. We were both relieved to break up."

Steph crossed her arms on the table and leaned forward, giving me her undivided attention. Her eyes were a warm hazel in the shady light of the patio. "I'm so sorry, Quinn. For so many things. I never realized you were thinking about getting engaged, even though I'd always pictured us together. Maybe that's why I was so devastated when you left me on that dive. It made me rethink everything." She reached over and took my hand. "This time, we're doing a better job of talking things through."

"Yeah, we are. And I feel like we're finally putting those bad memories in the past where they belong." I was ready for a subject change. "So it's back to work on Monday for you?"

"Uh-huh. Can't say I'm really looking forward to it."

I studied her face, her sharp nose and prominent cheekbones. As long as I'd known Steph, she'd been ambitious, graduating with a business degree and full of ideas of being self-employed. Yet that wasn't the direction she'd gone. "So how did the woman breathing fire to be an entrepreneur end up working in a cubicle for an insurance agency?"

She took a pull of beer and laughed, but it was humorless. "I guess both of us had lives that went sideways from what we expected, huh? I was devastated when I graduated and left, floundering. I moved to Tampa and got a job at Allied Insurance simply because they offered me a position with good pay and benefits. And somehow... I got stuck there. Turning thirty was a wake-up call. That was what made me decide to dive once more. To start *living*. And now I've met you again."

I held her gaze for a long moment, butterflies fluttering around my gut. I wasn't ready to end this—not by a long shot. "I'm taking Liam to Melody's next Saturday. I plan on letting her know about you and me."

Steph's eyes widened, and her lips curved into a pleased smile. "Really?"

I nodded, my chest tightening a little at the uncertainty in her voice. "Yeah. It'll make things easier going forward."

"How do you think she'll react?"

I shrugged, not really caring about my ex-wife's reaction. "She might be a little jealous. She always was where you were concerned." I laughed softly, remembering Melody's insecurities, which hadn't exactly faded over the years. When I called to inform her of my flight arrangements with Liam, she fished again for details about my new relationship. I told her I'd let her know when I was ready. And now I was. "We're far enough past the bitterness of the divorce now. We need to be able to co-parent without all that baggage. For Liam's sake."

"It's good that you both agree on putting him first."

"Besides," I said, my voice firming as I met her gaze. "I plan to make it crystal clear to Melody that you're a huge priority for me. I'm not hiding this—or you."

A flicker of doubt crossed her face, and she took a long swallow of beer, her gaze drifting toward the darkening ocean. "But what if it doesn't work, Quinn? What if Melody makes things difficult? What if—"

"Hey," I interrupted gently, lifting her chin with my finger so she met my eyes. "No *what ifs*. Melody realizes now that we weren't meant to be together. I don't think she'll make waves. We'll deal with whatever comes our way. Together. Okay?"

"Okay. I need you to know that I get it. But this is... uncharted territory for me, too."

I shot her a smile, trying to lighten the mood as I settled back in my seat. "So is cleaning turtle shells with me. But here we are. And so far, I'm liking where *here* is taking us."

A more confident smile raised her lips. "So do I."

An idea popped into my head. A fabulous idea. "After I drop off Liam at Melody's, how about if I swing by Tampa to see you? I could change my flight home to Monday morning."

Her eyes grew round, and a slow smile spread across her face. "You want to visit me?"

"Absolutely." In fact, I was getting more excited about the idea by the second.

"That would be amazing, Quinn. Thank you." She reached across the table and squeezed my hand, her touch sending a jolt of warmth through me. "You've made some huge strides reaching out to me these past few days. Letting me into your life, letting me get to know Liam. Now it's my turn to make a gesture."

She paused, biting her lower lip, and a flicker of doubt crossed her face. "I wasn't sure whether to bring this up. It's all so up in the air. But now I can't resist—"

Her phone chimed just then, and she grabbed it, her eyes widening as she read the notification. She barked out a delighted laugh. "Speak of the devil!"

Fingers flying, she opened up an email, a gasp escaping her lips as she read.

Now I was curious. "What's that all about?"

"Ha-ha! Tomorrow morning. That's perfect!"

Her enthusiasm was contagious, making me smile, though I was completely clueless about why she was so excited.

Steph sat up straight and put her phone on the table. Then she met my gaze, her smile fading as she became serious. "Remember when I told you I'd become a yoga instructor but never taught?"

I nodded encouragingly, no less perplexed.

"When I met you again, I was all kinds of mixed up. So I went to Fuchsia Flow to relax and kept going back. The instructor and I have become friends."

"Monica Crandall? I certified her."

"Yes, she told me. And she's a big fan of yours, by the way. She's really easy to talk to and helped me this week. Long story short—she's moving to Bali and wants me to take over as instructor at Fuchsia Flow."

I sat back in my chair. My heart skipped a beat, then marched on at a furious rhythm. Whatever I'd been expecting, it wasn't that. "Here? Permanently?"

Steph tapped her phone. "That was the email I got. Monica talked to the owner of Fuchsia Flow and got me an interview. It's set up for tomorrow morning!" The smile fell off her face as she became somber. "Quinn, you reached out by inviting me to Liam's game. And again, just now, by wanting to visit me in Tampa. We both hurt each other badly. I've only realized on this trip how much I hurt you. I want to make a gesture too—to show you *I'm* serious. This is only an interview, and I might not get the job. But if I do, we'll have a lot easier time seeing each other."

Tears came to my eyes, embarrassing me.

Why should I be embarrassed? Steph is the only person in the world I've ever felt comfortable showing my full range of emotions. Showing myself.

"They'd be idiots not to hire you."

Her smile was back, lighting up her face. There was no hesitancy in her posture or expression—she was fully committed. Hope lit in my body, soaring from my feet to my head.

"Monica said she thought the odds were really good," Steph continued. "Especially with her recommending me."

Her smile faded, another look coming over her face, one

I knew well. Desire filled her eyes, and all my blood headed to my core. "But we've got all evening and night before I need to worry about my interview. But I want you to know I'm doing everything possible to meet you halfway this time. More than halfway if I need to."

I blinked rapidly, still processing her news, then traced the soft skin of her forearm. I needed to touch her. "Me too. We'll make this work."

She grasped my hand and pressed her palm against mine. The movement sent a shiver dancing through my body as her warm, liquid eyes locked on mine. "We've lost eight years, Quinn. Let's not waste another minute."

At the same time, we stood. I pulled her into my arms, a movement both new and intimately familiar at the same time. I lowered my head, kissing her deeply, then picked her up in my arms. Her weight was easily distributed as I draped one arm under her back and the other under her knees. Effortless. Raw, pulsing arousal rocketed through me as I turned toward the house. "Let's go inside."

Chapter Twenty-Eight

Steph

AS QUINN CARRIED me toward his bedroom, I trailed a line of kisses across his neck and under his chin. He smelled of shaving cream and his skin was nearly smooth under my lips. He set me down inside his dim room and kicked the door shut with one foot. The blinds were closed, but afternoon light drifted in, letting me see the desire in his eyes.

Hot blood coursed through my veins as we came together. I kissed him fiercely as an urgent moan escaped my throat. I ripped his shirt over his head, tossing it aside in my haste to slide my hands up the flat, hard muscles of his back.

He was beautifully masculine. Hard, strong, and very solid.

And you're all mine...

"I've missed you, Quinn." I whispered the words into his ear, confident in saying them now.

He pulled back and cupped my face in both his hands,

staring at me evenly. "We've lost so much. Years. Experiences. Each other. I'm sorr—"

I silenced him with my fingers against his lips. "No more apologies. I know how you feel. I forgive you. I love you."

He gently pulled my hand away and kissed my palm. "I forgive you. And I love you too."

"Then let's start again. Right now."

He pulled my shirt over my head and had my bra off in moments. In a rush now, both of us slid off our shorts and underwear, standing before each other naked. Cupping both breasts in his hands, Quinn traced his thumbs over their peaks, then rubbed them firmly. Exactly how I liked it. I moaned, a sound full of longing and craving.

He took a step back and let his gaze wander slowly down my body. "I've always felt you were made for me. We fit together so well."

I smiled as I rubbed both hands over his broad, hard shoulders. "I'm glad we still do. Your body is a lot different now."

He arched a brow, a ghost of a smile appearing. "Is that a good thing or a bad thing?"

"My God. You're incredible." I took his hand and pressed it between my legs. "Can't you tell what you do to me?" I gasped as his fingers stroked me.

His voice was deep and thick with desire. "I think I have some idea. And I couldn't hide what you do to me if I wanted to."

I dropped to my knees before him. "No, you certainly can't."

He made a deep, guttural noise in his throat as I wrapped both hands around him, his skin so soft and silky. Enveloping him in my mouth, Quinn tipped his head back with a long, strangled groan, running both hands over the strands of my hair. I continued, intensely focused on how his breath deepened, becoming ragged. The knowledge of what I was doing to him, and the remembrance of what he enjoyed. Deep, pulsing waves traveled through me, settling firmly between my legs.

Then he took a step back and helped me to my feet. Quinn jerked me to him, grinding his hips against me, and lowered his head for a long, probing kiss. "If you don't get in that bed in the next five seconds, I might throw you in it."

I smiled, though I admitted the image of him throwing me into bed was enough to weaken my knees. "I'll climb in bed. But hold onto that thought for next time. We might have to try that out."

His sheets were cool under my hot skin and held the scent of fresh linen.

God, he even does laundry regularly. How was I stupid enough to let this guy go?

I almost laughed but smothered it by burying my face in his neck, not wanting to confuse him. Instead, I took a deep inhale of him, filling my lungs with Quinn. I felt almost giddy with happiness and desire. I kissed him hard, our lips smashing together, then nipped him lightly.

He pulled back with a smile. "Feisty, are we?"

"Very." Just having him so near made me squirm.

Quinn saw it and his smile changed, bare craving flooding into his eyes. "Well, let me see what I can do about that." Pulling my head back, he kissed below my jaw and down my neck, opening his mouth to lay a long, wet stripe until he reached my breast.

I arched my back, grabbing the back of his head and pulling him closer. He used his hand on my other breast to complement what he was doing with his mouth, and my chest was rising and falling with the force of my rapid breaths. Electricity charged through every cell of my body.

He continued downward, circling my navel with his tongue and watching me. I froze, caught in his intense, fiery gaze. Mesmerized as he moved lower yet. He commanded me with his eyes not to look away as he settled between my legs. Then he went to work. We continued staring at each other. Quinn's face was visible between my breasts, and it was the most erotic thing I'd ever seen. A shudder wracked me, a foreshock.

Quinn's eyes softened.

He's smiling!

Finally, I couldn't help myself, closing my eyes and tipping my head back as I cried out. We had never been like this.

Nothing had ever been like this.

I was already so turned on, my climax washed over me in no time. It built and built, extending in a long wave that I hoped would never end. I buried one hand in his short hair and scrunched the sheet with my other, twisting it. Short, moaning gasps escaped my mouth.

Yet we were a long way from finished.

Quinn lifted up and wiped his arm over his mouth. He climbed up the bed and opened the drawer of his nightstand, then pulled out a foil packet. He rolled on the condom, then stretched out on top of me. Faint light filtered through the room, enough to make out his chiseled, masculine features.

He pressed his mouth to my ear as he positioned himself between my legs. "Are you ready for me?"

Before I could answer the obvious, he slammed into me. I cried out and wrapped both legs around his waist, letting him in deeper. "Oh my God, Quinn."

He laughed softly, then lightened his action slightly, settling into a motion not quite so punishing.

Every nerve in my body was still alight. I could feel every square inch where our bodies met, where skin slid over skin as we became sweaty.

Pushing against his shoulders, I rolled on top and sat upright, straddling him. I rose and fell, dragging both hands through my hair as I arched my back.

Quinn's eyes were half-lidded as he stared at me, his breath now ragged. "Steph, you are the most glorious thing I've ever seen. Do that again."

I obliged, closing my eyes and fanning my hair out. I tossed it forward and leaned down, letting it brush over his chest.

Quinn groaned loudly, wrapping both arms around my torso and yanking me down to him. I kissed him hard, sliding my tongue in as he met me. He panted against my mouth, raw, primal sounds as his climax rose from what sounded like the depths of him. Quinn held me even more tightly to him, his strong arms enveloping me as he called my name.

We remained still for several minutes, and I could feel his heart beating against my chest, slowly returning to its regular rhythm. I stretched my legs out, nestling my head into the hollow of his neck. My eyelids grew heavy as he lightly stroked my back. I hardly felt solid, like my body was liquid and melting into him.

Eventually, Quinn spoke. "You're really going to move here?"

Bending my neck, I traced my lips softly over his pectoral muscle. "Yes. If I don't get the job at Fuchsia Flow, I'll find something else. We lost each other once, Quinn. We can't let it happen again."

I snuggled against him as his arms encircled me, cradling me within his strength. "We won't let it happen again. This time is for keeps, Steph."

I NERVOUSLY SMOOTHED my skirt as I walked across the lobby of the Coral Queen, my black pumps clicking on the tile floor. Finding business attire at a tropical resort was no easy feat, but I had located a high-end boutique and purchased a white blouse, black pencil skirt, and shoes. The outfit cost *way* too much money, but I really wanted to nail this interview.

I passed through a nondescript entryway with *Executive Offices* stenciled overhead and continued down a white hallway. At the end, a young woman sat behind a marble desk, the hotel logo on the wall behind her. She looked up at me with a smile.

"Hi. I'm Stephanie McIntyre. I've got an interview this morning for the position at Fuchsia Flow."

"Of course. Have a seat and I'll show you in when they're ready."

They're?

I sat in an armchair. In her email, Monica mentioned that she'd be at the interview but hadn't said anything about additional people. Within minutes, the young woman showed me into a small room where I sat in a blue-and-white fabric chair. Monica and another woman sat across a wooden coffee table in matching armchairs. Monica had dispensed with her Bali tops and wore a sharp Fuchsia Flow polo shirt.

The mystery woman appeared in her thirties and wore a rose-colored tailored suit. Her hair was swept into an elegant French roll. She nodded at me, a touch of regalness in the gesture. Right away, I understood I was looking at senior management.

"Thanks for joining us on such short notice," the woman said, her voice low-pitched. "I'm Jordan Michaels, the owner of the Coral Queen."

The last thing I had expected was the hotel owner to be in on my interview, but I put all the confidence I could into my smile. "Nice to meet you. And thank *you* for setting this up so quickly. I'm on the twelve-thirty ferry back to Miami."

"I admit I'm concerned about hiring someone with very little experience for this position. Fuchsia Flow is a small studio—you'd be the only yoga instructor and likely the only employee. At least to start."

I nodded. "I don't have much experience teaching yoga, but I've been taking classes for years. Plus, Monica gave me an audition," I added with a laugh. "I have a business degree and eight years' experience as a team leader at Allied Insurance."

Monica's lips rose into a smile. "I assured Jordan you'd be a great addition to the studio. You've got the instincts of how and why to correct yoga poses, and that's what counts. You can pick up the day-to-day running of the studio as you go."

After a grateful nod to Monica, I leaned forward in my chair and addressed Jordan. "I also should point out that I'm no stranger to the island. I grew up here, and I plan on staying. If you hire me, you shouldn't need to look for another instructor for a long time."

"I'm glad to hear that," Jordan said. She was professional and pleasant but gave nothing away. "Monica is hard to replace, and we're going to miss her. Let me ask you this:

What changes would you make to the studio to improve its profitability?"

My answer popped into my head immediately. It was a slight gamble—my idea could be taken as criticism of Monica. But I sensed Jordan was a shrewd businesswoman who appreciated confidence in a new hire. "I've taken several classes at Fuchsia Flow. It's a beautiful facility, and you're right—Monica is great. But there were very few other students in my classes. If you hired me, one of the first things I'd do would be to reach out to residents and staff workers on the island and offer discounted classes to them. The problem with only advertising the studio to guests is then you're at the mercy of hotel occupancy. Getting steady business from locals would even out income fluctuations."

Jordan arched a brow, a small smile rising on her face. "Monica made the same suggestion recently. Have you two been comparing notes?"

Monica laughed. "Not at all. And there's another benefit to the idea. If classes are busy, it reassures hotel guests that Fuchsia Flow is worthy of their limited vacation time." She turned slightly in her chair to look at Jordan. "Steph gets my full recommendation. She's had some difficulties during this trip and has shown resilience, courage, and a solid head on her shoulders. When she taught the mock class to me, she was calm and encouraging. I think she'd be great in the position."

I nodded and tried to look demure and interested, while inside my heart soared at Monica's words.

After a nod, Jordan looked me straight in the eye. "Then I guess only one question remains. When can you start?"

Chapter Twenty-Nine

Steph

THE HOT MIDDAY sun beat down on me as I stepped onto the wooden dock and checked my watch. Again. I headed toward the tropical-themed ferry, pulling my roller suitcase behind me. I had purposely not texted Quinn about getting the job since we would see each other before I left, and I wanted to surprise him.

Except it was closing in on 12:30 and he wasn't here yet.

The ferry dock was a fair distance from where the dive boat moored, so I couldn't tell whether *Aqua Dreams* had returned from the morning trip.

Come on, Quinn. Hurry up!

With solid plans to meet after he dropped off Liam, I wasn't worried about him standing me up for our farewell. No, Quinn and I worked through our problems. We'd said a proper goodbye that morning in bed, before he had to pick up Liam and I had to prepare for my interview.

But I was dying to see him one final time. The dive boat

usually got back by noon, though some days it went to sites farther afield and got back later. Apparently, today was one of those days.

I stopped before the ferry, craning my head toward the boat slips, as if searching could make Quinn appear.

"You coming aboard?"

I turned. The speaker was Lance, the ferryman. His face politely inquiring, his loud, tropical-print shirt covered in flamingos on the wing looked like it might take flight at any moment.

"Yeah. I was waiting to say goodbye to someone, but I'd better get on board."

He took my suitcase and I stepped aboard, disappointment twisting in my stomach.

Guess I'll just have to call him tonight after I get back to Tampa.

Passing several other guests, I moved toward the bench at the stern of the boat and took a seat, ducking past several plastic palm trees attached to the side of the canopy. Lance hopped onto the dock, bending over a line wrapped around a metal cleat. I glanced at the cooler, contemplating a final goodbye glass of champagne.

"Hold on! Wait a second, Lance!"

I snapped my head around at Quinn's shout, a grin splitting my face as he sprinted down the dock toward us. He was impossible to miss in his white rash guard and tie-dyed board shorts. Skidding to a stop, he grabbed the ferry railing with one hand and vaulted over it, tucking his legs to one side. He landed lightly on the wooden deck of the boat, his eyes searching passengers until he found me.

"Uh, hi, Quinn," Lance said, the line in one hand, and his brow lined.

"How's it going, Lance?" Quinn replied without looking. His head froze as he made eye contact with me. "Be with you in a second. Don't untie yet, okay?"

The half dozen guests on the ferry ducked for the covered interior as the large form of Quinn slid by. "S'cuze me, sorry, pardon."

He stared intensely at me, moving with strong purpose. The sight of him sent butterflies fluttering around my stomach. I rose from the bench and stepped into the aisle, my grin growing as he neared. Unsmiling, Quinn marched toward me without slowing. I couldn't help taking a step backward, and my knees bumped the rear panel of the boat.

When Quinn reached me, he wrapped both arms around my torso and bent me over backward in his arms. Cheers went up from the assembled guests as his lips met mine. And stayed there, though he was breathing hard after his run to the ferry. Pressing a hand to his face, I kissed him back, soaking in his presence.

Eventually, he stood me back upright. No doubt the smile on my face was dazed, and his kiss had left me slightly breathless. Heat flooded my face as I acknowledged the applauding crowd, though Quinn just laughed as he gave them a casual wave. We moved to a rear corner where we had a little privacy.

Quinn grinned broadly. "Wasn't sure I was going to get here in time."

"Me neither! We were right about to take off."

"Well? How was the interview?"

My goofy smile turned even fuller, and excitement flooded through me. "I got the job! Jordan hired me on the spot, so I'll start looking for an apartment soon."

With excitement lighting up his face, Quinn cupped my cheeks and kissed me again. "This is really happening, right?"

My face stung as my grin tried to take up permanent residence. "Oh, yes. Don't doubt me now, Quinn."

He laughed again and boosted me up to eye level. "When do you start?"

"Within a month! Monica is moving to Bali in six weeks, so that will give us a little overlap before she goes. We plan on keeping in touch."

"Maybe we can vacation in Bali sometime." He waggled his eyebrows. "The diving is supposed to be great there, and it sounds very romantic, you know."

"Hold onto that thought."

As he deposited me back onto the deck, his smile fell. "Yeah. Next weekend is going to be rough. Gotta get through that first. I talked some more with Liam about it on the way to school this morning."

I cocked my head. "About what, specifically?"

"Reassuring him that even though things might be different when he comes back this fall, they'll be better than ever." He burst into laughter. "He asked if I was finally willing to admit you were my girlfriend."

"Oh? And what did you say?"

"I told him that was exactly what you are." He glanced around at the passengers enjoying their last glasses of champagne. "Thank God I didn't miss you. The last thing I want is you thinking I'm turning my back on you. Never again, Steph."

Tears pricked at the corner of my eyes. "I believe you. Ten days, Quinn. That was all it took for our lives to completely change."

He nodded. "Telling Melody about you face-to-face won't be easy. But I'm determined to make it work. For Liam, and for you. You're worth some awkward conversations."

"Good luck. I know it won't be easy next weekend. But I'll be there when it's over."

"Quinn!" Lance called out, still standing on the dock. He held both arms out wide, his ruddy face frowning. "I've got to shove off, man. You coming or going?"

Quinn gave him a quick wave before returning his attention to me. "I'd better leave. I'll see you soon?"

"I can't wait. I miss you already."

"I love you, Steph."

"Love you too."

And after one final short, but very thorough, kiss, Quinn passed the guests again and hopped back onto the dock. He clapped Lance on the shoulder, thanking him as he passed, then continued down the dock. I watched him go, his stride athletic and confident, and a part of my heart reserved only for him panged at our parting. At the entrance to the wooden walkway, Quinn turned one final time and waved. A smile stretched my lips as I returned it.

In another moment, he was gone.

I retook my seat on the bench, same as on my outbound trip. Lance steered us into the canal and back toward the mainland. I glanced around for any stowaway crabs that might be aboard, but this time there weren't any. As warm sunlight sparkled on the water, I couldn't help shaking my head at how different I was than the last time I rode this ferry. How drastically different my life was. Next weekend felt like the final hurdle.

After one final glance at Sandpiper Cay, I studied the ocean. I smiled as a flying fish launched out of the surface, gliding more than twenty feet before splashing back into the sea.

Back to home.

Just like how Quinn and I—and Liam—belonged here

on Sandpiper Cay. Melody might not be my favorite person in the world, but if Quinn was willing to stand up for me, I sure as hell would for him. I would be a part of Liam's life, not just Quinn's.

Melody might not like that Quinn and I were together, but she'd have to accept it.

Chapter Thirty

Quinn

A GATE AGENT droned on about a departing flight as Liam and I walked down the concourse, and my stomach twisted into a tight knot. The Destin airport was small and bustling, filled with vacationers in bright clothes. Despite trying to stay upbeat for Liam, sadness was a lead weight in my gut. I glanced down at my son, who walked silently beside me, his head ducked and his shoulders slumped. He clutched the stuffed sea turtle I'd given him this morning before we left the house.

"You okay, buddy?" I asked, resting a hand on his shoulder.

Liam nodded, but his lower lip trembled. "What if Craig doesn't like me? Because they live together now."

Guilt stabbed at me. It was one thing to tell myself—and Steph—that Liam would be fine, that kids were resilient. But seeing the worry etched on his face brought the reality home. Stopping, I crouched down so I was eye-to-eye with him.

"Liam," I said firmly, "Craig *does* like you a lot. And their living together doesn't change that. Your mom can't wait to see you."

Liam chewed on his bottom lip, those big blue eyes—so much like mine—welling up.

"Hey," I said gently, wiping away a stray tear that escaped while trying to hold it together myself. "It's going to be okay. You're going to have a great time with Mom—she's got lots of great stuff planned for you guys. We'll talk on the phone as much as possible."

He nodded, sniffling, and I pulled him into a hug. He was getting so big, but in that moment, he was just my sweet little boy.

"It's gonna be okay, buddy," I murmured before kissing the top of his head.

As we pulled apart, he gave me a brave nod. I forced a smile, hoping it reached my eyes. "Come on, let's go see Mom."

I stood, my heart aching. Leading Liam by the hand, we rounded a corner and entered the baggage claim area. My heart leaped into my throat. Melody stood near the carousels, talking with a clean-cut, dark-haired man. From across the room, I recognized Craig. His back was to us, but Melody's head was on a swivel, her blonde hair swishing around her shoulders. Her gaze swept the crowd, then she spotted us. Her expression softened, and she waved.

Liam let go of my hand and took off at a run, his earlier anxieties forgotten. "Mom!"

The tightness in my chest eased a little as I watched Liam launch himself into Melody's arms. She scooped him up, laughing, and held him close. "Oh, my little guy! You've grown so much!"

As I approached, Craig shook my hand. His grip was medium, not trying to get into a pissing contest with me. I nodded back cordially and said hello.

"Hey there, Liam! Good to see you, buddy," Craig said, holding out a hand for a high-five. After Melody released him, Liam grinned and slapped his palm against it.

Maybe this wasn't going to be so bad after all.

As Liam and Craig began discussing the massive fish tank against the wall, I turned to Melody.

"Hey," I said, trying for a casual tone, though a fine sweat had broken out on my back at the news I was about to deliver.

"Hey yourself." Melody's smile was hesitant, but her eyes held a warmth that surprised me. "It's good to see you, Quinn. You look..." She paused, her gaze sweeping over me, "tan and healthy."

"Thanks. It's been good to be home," I said. We stood there awkwardly for a moment as arrival announcements sounded overhead. Liam was pointing at something in the fish tank, and Craig leaned down, listening intently.

"Liam seems to have adjusted well to Sandpiper Cay," Melody said. "He's been quiet about coming to visit, but his greeting now was reassuring."

"Yeah, he's doing well, and he's excited to spend time with you. But there will be an adjustment every time he goes back and forth. It'll get easier as he gets older." I took a deep breath, pointing with my head off to the side. "I'd like to talk to you for a second. Now's a good time since we're waiting for his luggage."

She followed me as we stopped in front of a large display of a white sand beach. "Let me guess. Is this about your new woman?"

"Yeah. I wanted to talk to you in person and get everything in the open."

"Well, that sounds mysterious. And maybe ominous. Do I know her?"

I met her hazel eyes squarely—not being aggressive, but not backing down, either. "Yes. I'm seeing Steph again."

Surprise darted over Melody's face, followed by an expression I knew well from her. Envy. Then she took a deep breath and schooled her face. "Stephanie McIntyre?"

I frowned. "Of course."

Her eyes darted to the tile floor. "Okay. Your new flame is your old flame. Again."

I consciously kept my posture relaxed, though my pulse was skittering right along. "We reconnected when she came to Sandpiper Cay recently."

Melody gave me a long, evaluating stare. "How serious is it?"

"Serious enough to tell you about it."

She nodded slowly before taking a deep breath, still processing. "I'm not going to lie, Quinn. It's a little weird. It's been a long time, but..." She trailed off, her expression unreadable.

"But?" I prompted, my anxiety increasing.

Melody gave a small, self-deprecating laugh. "Maybe it's a little ego-bruising that you two are back together? Like you and I were just a... blip in your lives. A parenthesis." She shook her head, as if trying to dismiss the thought. "Which is ridiculous, of course. Our marriage was anything but a blip, and we got Liam out of it. But I'm not surprised you and Steph found your way back to each other."

"I'm glad you feel this way." I studied her, seeing a new maturity in her expression. And a new confidence. This was a different Melody. A better Melody.

"Well, now I know," she said, her tone lighter now. "So what are your plans? Is Steph moving to Sandpiper Cay?"

I nodded. "She's taking over as a yoga instructor at Fuchsia Flow."

Melody blinked rapidly. "You guys have it all figured out. Quinn, isn't this all a bit... sudden?"

"Sudden in some ways, and inevitable in others."

She glanced at Liam, then back to me. "Listen, I need to be honest with you. This... whole situation is going to take some adjusting to. For me, for Liam. But I'm willing to make it work. You and I have to get along. For him."

I relaxed enough to give her a small smile. "Thanks. I feel the same way. There's one more thing..."

"What's that?"

"Steph is going to be a part of Liam's life. A real part. She's not some woman I only spend time with when he's not with me." I started to prop my hands on my hips, then dropped them again, not wanting to come across too aggressive. I was walking a tightrope here trying to work this all out.

Melody's eyes narrowed slightly, but then she surprised me by laughing. "Quinn, believe me, I get it. I'm not a monster. I knew when I left that you'd eventually move on. I'm doing the same with Craig, and you've got no complaints about that, right?"

"No. He seems like a good guy."

"He is," Melody said firmly. "Steph and I have some not-so-great history, but maybe it's time to leave all that behind. We'll take things slowly, okay?"

I nodded, respecting her request and damn relieved at how grown up she was being about this. "Fair enough. And we'll talk to Liam before he comes home. Make sure he understands what's happening."

Melody smiled, and this time it reached her eyes. "Sounds good. This really is like something out of a movie, isn't it? You and Steph. All these years later."

I smiled back. "Yeah, I guess it is."

As the carousel rumbled to life and baggage appeared on it, all four of us returned to watch for Liam's blue suitcase. When it appeared, a hard ball lodged in my throat. I pulled it off and set it next to Craig, then did my best not to cry when I glanced down at my son.

"It's time to go already?" he asked, his voice small. He pulled his stuffed turtle in tighter.

"I know, buddy. I wish we had more time, too." I knelt down and pulled him into another hug, his small arms clinging tightly around my neck. "But my flight to Tampa leaves in an hour."

"Don't forget to call me," Liam said, his voice muffled against my shirt.

"I won't. We'll catch up on all the fun you're about to have. I love you."

"Love you too, Dad."

I stood, trying to ignore the lead weight in my chest as Melody put a hand on Liam's shoulder and Craig lifted his suitcase. The trio headed toward the exit. Liam looked back once and waved, a bittersweet smile on his face. I waved back, forcing a smile of my own. The exit doors closed silently behind them.

I took several huge breaths to collect myself, and it was probably a good thing I didn't have time to linger. I headed to security and passed though in a haze, my movements automatic and unthinking. At the gate, I sat in the corner to wait for my flight to Tampa to board. I did my best to concentrate on the positive—that I was on my way to visit the woman who was the love of my life.

Because the only alternative was to think that I was leaving my son behind. I checked my watch, willing the minutes to pass.

Chapter Thirty-One

Steph

AT THE SOUND of the doorbell's ring, my heart leaped into my throat. I smoothed down my sundress and ran a hand through my hair, double-checking my reflection in the mirror. Pleased with what I saw, I opened the door. Quinn stood there, even taller and broader than I remembered. He looked exhausted, shadows under his eyes and his shoulders slumped. Sadness was a palpable weight surrounding him.

"Oh, sweetie. Come on in," I said softly, moving aside so he could enter.

After stepping through the doorway, Quinn dropped his duffel bag on the floor and yanked me into his arms. He held me so tightly I could barely breathe, but I didn't care. I wrapped my arms around his waist, burying my face in his chest. He smelled faintly of spice and the clean scent of his clothes. Familiar and comforting, but now I needed to do the comforting. I slid my hands up his back in broad sweeps, just letting him exist with me.

As he held me, the tension drained from his shoulders. I

pulled my head back and framed his face with my hands to brush a gentle, soft kiss over his lips. Quinn clung to me, eventually breaking the kiss to rest his forehead against mine.

"It's okay to be sad," I murmured. "You wouldn't be human if you weren't feeling this."

"I know. It's just rough saying goodbye." He let out a long sigh, then pulled away to meet my gaze. A slow smile spread across his face, erasing the sadness. "But being here with you..." He trailed off, then skated his thumb slowly across my jawline. "This is exactly what I need."

I gazed into those pale blue eyes, now not so sad. "I just opened a bottle of wine. Want a glass?"

"God, yes." He glanced around curiously as we made our way to the kitchen. "Nice place."

My apartment wasn't fancy, but it was comfortable and colorful, with artwork I'd collected over the years. It gave off eclectic and comforting vibes. Or at least that was how it had felt until I'd returned from Sandpiper Cay. Now, seeing it through Quinn's eyes, it felt a little small and... safe.

A little too much like the life I was leaving behind.

"Thanks. I've given my move-out notice and started packing." I poured us both a generous glass of cabernet and handed one to Quinn. "I was just about to start dinner. Pasta with pesto sauce."

"Sounds good." He took a sip of wine and smiled. "Want some help?"

"Sure. Grab the tomatoes out of the fridge, would you?"

We fell into an easy rhythm as we worked side-by-side in the small kitchen. I chopped vegetables, and Quinn manned the stove. Unsurprisingly, he soon outpaced me in the culinary department. It was obvious this wasn't his first attempt at pesto.

"You are so good at this," I said, watching as he toasted pine nuts for the salad in a skillet, the rich scent of them filling the air.

"Thanks." His eyes crinkled at the corners as he smiled. "It's become a necessity, with Liam around. Hot dogs with mac and cheese only goes so far."

I laughed, remembering our college days when he refused to attempt anything beyond ramen noodles. "I'm glad you're here, even if it's only for the one time."

When he looked over at me, the levity had vanished from his eyes. "Only one time at this apartment, but there's lots more to come." Before I could reply, he leaned down, and his lips captured mine in a soft kiss that coaxed a moan from me. His kiss only made me crave the connection we'd rekindled. Before we could get too carried away, I took a firm step back.

"Uh, Quinn?" I said, my voice a little breathless. "The garlic needs to be minced."

A broad grin rose on his face. "Right. Garlic. Important detail."

He reached for the clove sitting on a cutting board, and we went back to preparing dinner. As Quinn minced the garlic, I checked him out from the corner of my eye. He had a way of filling up a room, even my small kitchen.

He caught me staring and winked. "Something catch your eye?"

Heat crept up my cheeks, and I quickly turned back to the tomatoes I was slicing. "Just admiring your, uh, garlic-mincing technique. Very impressive."

He laughed softly. "I've got a few other techniques for you to enjoy," he murmured, his voice low and suggestive.

My breath caught, a wave of heat coursing through me. "I'm counting on it."

We finished preparing dinner, the conversation between us now charged with a delicious tension. As the pasta cooked, Quinn refilled our glasses, and we moved out to the balcony. The evening air was warm and humid.

We sat side-by-side on the cushion covering my wrought-iron bench, sipping our wine as the last of the day's light faded. The warmth of his leg pressed against mine, and I leaned my head against his shoulder, unable to resist.

He wrapped his arm around me to pull me closer. "This feels good. *Right*."

"We fit together so well," I agreed, closing my eyes and letting myself savor the moment. Being with Quinn again felt like coming home.

We ate dinner at a small table near the kitchen window, and the savory aroma of pesto filled the air. Quinn recounted his conversation with Melody at the airport, and the tightness in my stomach slowly dissolved as I realized Melody might have grown a little over the years too. While I doubted she and I would ever be friends, maybe there was room to be cordial to each other.

"So," he said, his face full of expectation, "Have you set a date to move yet?"

I smiled back, excitement racing through me. "Not yet, but I'm almost there. I gave my notice at Allied today and I plan to move to Sandpiper Cay as soon as possible. I've already found an apartment online."

"That's incredible, Steph." I raised my hand to rest against his cheek as he leaned across the table and kissed me. "I can't tell you how happy that makes me. You coming back to Sandpiper Cay. Us being together again... It feels like fate, you know?"

"That's exactly what it is," I agreed, and my heart swelled with a happiness I hadn't felt in years.

. . .

Later, as we lay together in my bed, a contented sigh escaped my lips. Quinn shifted and pulled me closer to his sweaty chest. The intoxicating scent of him filled my senses. Outside, the night was alive with the sounds of the city. But here, nothing else existed except the two of us.

"You feel so good," he murmured against my temple.

I stretched luxuriously. "So do you."

We lay in comfortable silence as I listened to the steady beat of his heart against my chest. It was a rhythm I could get used to. "It's hard to believe how much has happened in such a short time."

Quinn slowly stroked his fingers over my back. "I never thought... I never dared to hope we'd find our way back to each other."

"Me neither. But I'm so glad we did."

I snuggled closer and fit myself against him, just like I always had. The thought of leaving for Sandpiper Cay and starting my new life filled me with excitement and a touch of apprehension. I was leaving behind a familiar life, a successful career. But I was also leaving behind loneliness. And a rut a mile wide.

"It's a little scary, starting over," I admitted.

Quinn tightened his hold momentarily, his touch reassuring. "I know. But you won't be alone. I'll be there, every step of the way. And Liam, too, when he gets back."

I smiled, picturing the three of us living on Sandpiper Cay. "I can't wait to get started."

Chapter Thirty-Two

Steph

FOUR MONTHS LATER

I stood at the entrance of the Fuchsia Flow studio, saying goodbye as people filed out. A middle-aged, heavyset woman stopped as others flowed around her. A glittery pink headband pulled her brown curls back from her face, which bounced as she shook her head. "Thank you for all the help during class. I felt like one of the hippos in tutus in *Fantasia*."

I gave her a warm smile, sympathizing with how difficult yoga could be for beginners. "You did great! Don't be so hard on yourself. This class was a big improvement over yesterday."

"I'll keep pecking away at it. See you tomorrow." The woman joined the line in the lobby waiting at the glass counter to sign the room charge.

I breathed a satisfied sigh at another busy, successful day. A month ago, I hired Willow as a receptionist and assistant. After advertising Fuchsia Flow to residents of Sandpiper Cay and offering a thirty-percent discount, classes quickly filled up. Soon I had more business than I could handle. I also made sure resort guests on the island were aware of the facility, and the studio might soon need a second yoga instructor to expand our hours.

Speaking of time...

I glanced at my watch and confirmed I needed to get moving. Heading into the back hall, I opened a metal locker and grabbed my street clothes, a T-shirt and cargo shorts. After ducking into the restroom to change, I headed out the back door into the alley. The executive wing of the Coral Queen lay on the other side, and I thought back to my interview for the position.

At the time, I hadn't understood how rare it was for Jordan Michaels to interview someone in person. I'd hardly seen the hotel owner since, as the woman preferred to keep a low profile. But right from the start, Jordan had put her full faith and trust in me to manage Fuchsia Flow. In the three months of my employment, I had already increased the studio's bottom line. Monica had done an excellent job getting the studio off the ground, but my business acumen was needed to move it to the next level. Not to mention fulfilling my college dream of my own successful business. I might not own Fuchsia Flow, but the decisions were all mine.

I climbed in my golf cart, tossed my backpack in the rear seat, and headed toward Portsmouth. It was nearly 4:00 p.m. and Lance's high-speed ferry was snugly tied to the main dock. I continued along Main Street, bumping along as the asphalt road changed to sand. On my right was one of the main residential blocks for permanent residents, including the three-story structure that housed my one-bedroom apartment.

But I passed by it, instead turning left, and headed toward the large green field in the distance. I parked next to several other golf carts and exited, joining the small crowd assembled at the side of the field. Two soccer goals lay at opposite ends of the pitch and a man with chocolate skin and tightly cropped black hair stood in front of the group of watching people.

He studied the children on the field intently before blowing a silver whistle in his mouth, then let it fall. "Come on, kids! Get after the ball." Jerome spoke with a soft melodious accent and liked to tease Quinn that he'd been strong-armed into becoming a coach.

Which was laughable because Jerome was one of the few Sandpiper Cay residents who were bigger than Quinn. He saw me arrive and nodded. "Afternoon. We're about finished."

"No rush." Shading my eyes with one hand, I peered at Liam. He passed the ball to the midfielder and stayed in formation as they traveled down the field. As they closed in on the goal, the girl passed him the ball back and Liam kicked it hard into the goal. He eased to a stop, exchanging a high five with the girl who had given him the assist.

I smiled. I'd been slightly shocked when Quinn returned with him several weeks ago. Over the summer with his mother, Liam had shot up like a weed and returned sporting a new look. Quinn and I had decided it would be best for Quinn to meet him alone, so he could update Liam on our relationship before arriving home. Melody had flown with the boy to Miami and Quinn picked him up there.

As thrilled as Quinn had been to see Liam again, he'd

been less pleased at the boy's new buzz cut. As they rode the ferry to Sandpiper Cay, Liam explained his mother had wanted the haircut shortly before he'd left.

Later, after the three of us had eaten dinner and Liam was unpacking in his room, a scowling Quinn had told me about it. "Melody wanted a parting shot, I guess. Good thing hair grows out. He won't be getting a cut for a while."

"He does look less like you without much hair."

Quinn crossed his arms. "That was her idea, I'm sure. No way. That dude is my Mini-Me."

I laughed, not about to disagree with him. Fortunately, Liam also considered himself Quinn's Mini-Me and wanted to grow the cut out. Quinn saw the humor in the situation and laughed with me, shaking his head.

The transition to having Liam back full-time had been an adjustment for both Quinn and me. All summer we had been nearly inseparable, either staying at his house or my apartment, and our relationship had steadily deepened. But after Liam's return, we spent the first seven nights apart, wanting him to adjust to the life he'd been used to the previous year. Then I stayed overnight, making a big break-fast with Quinn on a Saturday morning. Liam took it all in stride, and I'd stayed over more since.

After a few ball-passing drills, Jerome blew his whistle with two sharp blasts. "Okay, guys. That's a wrap. See you at the ferry on Saturday. Eight a.m. sharp! Don't be late!"

Liam laughed with his friend Grayson, and they walked off the field together. Spotting me, he waved and headed my way.

"I saw your goal," I said as we headed toward my golf cart. "You moved the ball great. Your pass to Olivia was perfect."

"Thanks. I think the drills we've been practicing in the backyard are paying off."

Over the past month, Liam and I had bonded further over our shared experience with soccer. Though more than a little rusty, the motions had soon come back to me, and I worked one-on-one with him regularly.

We pulled into the driveway of Quinn's house and headed inside.

"I'm going to take a shower," Liam said and headed toward his bedroom.

I went to the kitchen and opened the fridge, scoping out possibilities for dinner. Though Quinn was the much better cook, I tried to help out when I could. My email dinged on my phone, and when I saw it was from Monica, I rushed to open it.

Leaning on the counter and resting my elbows on the laminate surface, I practically salivated over the photos Monica had included. I was examining a picture of an intricate Balinese temple carving when the front door opened. Quinn walked into the kitchen, his pale blue eyes lighting up when he saw me.

Taking me in his arms, he lowered to kiss me. Prepared for a quick peck hello, I was surprised when he deepened the kiss, opening his mouth for a long, leisurely tour of my mouth. My blood thrummed through my veins when he finally released me. "Wow. That was quite the hello."

"I heard the shower running and figured we were safe from being interrupted." He whisked his lips over me again. "How was your day?"

"Great. The studio is really doing well. Did your student do okay?"

Quinn was teaching an older open water scuba student

who had been palpably nervous to start. She'd hardly been able to assemble her scuba kit with her shaking hands. But extra sessions had increased her confidence, and Quinn was deliberate and reassuring with her.

"Yeah. We finished up the pool sessions just now. I'll spread her open water checkouts over three days instead of two to make sure she feels confident."

I stroked a finger over his chin, his scruff prickly under my finger. "You're a fantastic instructor. I wonder if she knows how lucky she is. I know."

Smiling, he kissed my forehead. Then the photos on my phone distracted him, and he scrolled through several. "Nice. What's this?"

"Monica sent more pictures of Bali. She's working at a resort called Haven on the east coast of the island." I picked up the phone and laughed at the email. "She wants us both to know they have a dive shop on site and the resort is a wonderfully romantic place to visit."

He arched a brow, a speculative gleam entering his eye. "Maybe we'll need to think about that someday. I could see us in Bali."

"You wouldn't have to twist my arm!"

Liam entered, looking freshly scrubbed, and his hair wet. "Hi, Dad. I'm starving."

"Well, I don't want you wasting away on the kitchen floor. Too much mess to clean up."

Liam giggled, which brought a smile to my face. When the boy smiled, his resemblance to Quinn was even more remarkable.

"I was looking for dinner ideas when the email distracted me," I said.

"There's some hamburger meat in the bottom drawer." Quinn looked at Liam and rubbed his hands together.

"How about Quinn Douglas Special Hamburgers for dinner?"

"Yeah! I'll get the chips." Liam skipped to the pantry and opened the door while Quinn and I got busy preparing dinner. Just a normal evening.

Chapter Thirty-Three

Quinn

LATER THAT NIGHT, after Liam had gone to bed, Steph and I sat on a couch on my patio. I poured more wine into our glasses, smiling as crickets chirped in the still air around us. Lifting mine, I settled back and draped my arm over the back of the couch. I pulled Steph closer, leaning over to breathe in the scent of her tropical shampoo. The entire setting, and the steady *routine* of it filled me with peace.

My life was remarkably different than a year ago. Twelve months ago, I had been lonely but determined to make a new start. Trying to be the best father possible to a shaken, unruly son whose life had been upended. Now Liam was happy living on Sandpiper Cay. He'd had a good time with his mother but confessed when I picked him up that he was ready to leave. My heart had pounded in my chest when Liam said he wanted to *come home*.

I softly stroked Steph's long hair, still hardly able to believe that we were back together. That she'd been willing to give up her life in Tampa so we could have another chance.

"You took a big risk moving here," I said softly.

She turned to look at me, moonlight reflecting in her eyes. "Maybe, but there are times when you have to take risks. And I've learned that regret is worse."

I nodded. "I hear you there." I held up my glass. "To no regrets."

Our glasses clinked, a soft chime in the balmy night, and Steph settled closer to me, nestling against my shoulder. "There have been a lot of changes for us over the last year. A lot of great changes. I wonder what next year will bring."

Smiling, I kissed the top of her head. "I don't know exactly, but I'm confident whatever the future holds for us, our little family will come through with flying colors." I poked her playfully in the shoulder. "Maybe next year will bring a trip to Bali."

"Over the summer sometime? That would work better with Liam already at his mother's."

"Sounds great. You know, I imagine Bali would be a pretty nice place for a honeymoon."

She turned a full smile to me. "It would be a *great* place for a honeymoon."

I picked up her left hand, running my thumb over her bare ring finger. "Then we might have to go ring shopping sometime. I have a feeling it will go better this time."

Her smile faded, and she pressed her hand to my cheek. "When the time comes, I *know* it will go better, Quinn."

Steph resettled against me. I exhaled a long, contented sigh, confident we were both on the same page regarding the future. I rubbed her finger again.

Someday soon, Steph, my ring will be on your finger...

A soft breeze rustled a nearby tree that was in bloom,

bathing us in its heavenly scent. I took a deep breath, then lowered my head to plant a kiss on Steph's head. I pressed my cheek to the soft strands of her hair and smiled as a meteor streaked across the sky. I didn't even need to make a wish.

I was already living my dream.

Epilogue

Steph

THE FOLLOWING AUGUST

BEHIND QUINN'S HEAD, the sky was painted in pink and lavender as I stared up at him. My heart was so full my ribs felt tight, like I couldn't take a deep breath. His eyes were soft as he stared at me, full of deep love, along with a touch of wonder.

"You may kiss the bride," the pastor said.

Twitching the side of his mouth, Quinn lowered his head, moving his hand to gently cradle the back of my neck. He pressed his lips against mine.

A soft meeting of two sets of lips, the promise of a second chance fulfilled.

The small crowd applauded and cheered as we broke apart. Happy tears came to my eyes, but I blinked them away. Moving to stand by Quinn's side, I regripped my bouquet of pink and white roses. The smile on my face was completely beyond my control, a happiness unlike anything I'd ever known.

Behind Quinn, Liam stood in a matching charcoal gray tuxedo, a black pillow—now empty—cradled in both hands. His face showed palpable relief as he met my eyes. I winked and gave him a thumbs-up, making sure he knew he had been a stellar ring bearer. He shot me a crooked smile back, so similar to his father's.

The pastor took a breath behind me. "Ladies and gentlemen, I present Quinn and Stephanie Douglas!"

Laughing at the proclamation, I turned to look at Quinn again, and we shared another kiss. His mouth was impossibly soft under mine before he pulled back with a wink. He was magnificent in his gray tux. He and Liam wore light-blue bow ties that matched the hue of their eyes.

We stood in a nearly hidden garden, part of the Coral Queen. Not wanting the crowd of gawkers a beach wedding would surely attract, this private setting was perfect. Tall hedges surrounded a neat green lawn. Several rows of white chairs stood behind a white trellis arching over the bride and groom. White strings of party lights crossed overhead, and soft music emanated from hidden speakers.

Our wedding was an intimate affair. Liam was the only attendant, and my parents had come over from the mainland. A few of their friends from the island were in attendance along with Brenda and Bruce Douglas. Jana sat dabbing her eyes with a tissue.

A single long table sat off to one side and Quinn ushered me toward it, pressing his hand against the small of my back. I wore a white strapless wedding dress, the bodice embellished with scrolling flowers embroidered in white thread. We took our seats at the center of the table and accepted glasses of champagne from a waiter.

A glorious warmth radiated through me as Quinn leaned over to whisper in my ear. "Well, now we've done it. No going back now."

I stared into those blue eyes. "There was no going back for me quite a while ago."

Quinn had proposed during one of my yoga classes, of all things. One morning in March, he'd said he felt bad for not understanding better what I did for a living. Then he announced he'd be attending the 4:00 p.m. session.

He pointed an index finger at me. "But you have to promise not to laugh at me. I've never done yoga in my life."

I grinned and assured him he'd do fine. But halfway through the class, I was beginning to wonder. Quinn wasn't only new to the poses, he was huge and lumbering, almost falling over during the tree pose. Laughing, he returned to the pose, determined to master it. Fortunately, the rest of the class, nearly all women, thought he was very touching. They gave him their full support and encouragement as I repositioned him.

Over and over.

When the class was nearly over, I walked up to him yet again, trying to be as supportive as possible as I corrected his warrior one pose. He really was a sweetheart, but I was surprised he was having so much difficulty when he was such a naturally athletic man. "Widen your stance, sweetie. You'll have better balance if your feet aren't so close together."

Quinn dropped his hands to his sides and breathed out a long, drawn-out sigh. "I might need to admit that yoga isn't for me." Grinning, he shook his head at the chorus of disagreeing encouragement from the other women in the class. I was inhaling a breath to agree with them when he interrupted, the smile falling from his face. "But I do know one thing that *is* for me."

And he lowered to one knee and pulled a crushed-velvet box from a pocket of his shorts. Opening it, he presented an engagement ring and asked me to marry him. The women around us positively swooned.

My knees went weak. We had been talking about marriage and starting a family but hadn't decided anything. I had to give him credit for ingenuity.

Raising both hands to my mouth, I laughed and nodded. "Yes!"

Later, he informed me the ring was a loaner the jewelry store had given him. So we could pick out the real thing together.

At long last.

I admired the rings on my left hand. The engagement ring was a one-carat solitaire, and the matching wedding band wound around it intricately. Quinn had picked out a white gold band with a small, inlaid diamond.

Liam sat on Quinn's other side, eagerly watching as the waitstaff served us sirloin steak. He would spend that night with Quinn's parents while we occupied the honeymoon suite at the Coral Queen.

And in two days, we would take Liam back to his mother's for the remainder of the summer. I was also going this time to support Quinn. As his wife, I wanted to establish a presence with Melody. Never as Liam's mother—I knew better than that. But as an important person in his life, nonetheless.

The sky faded to black as the meal progressed. The cake was delectable, white with a cream cheese ribbon between layers. And neither Quinn nor I smashed it into each other's faces.

I was looking at the starlit sky when the moon peeked out from behind a cloud. "What a perfect night."

Quinn's eyes smoldered as he leaned over to whisper, "It's hardly started yet."

I matched his expression. "I can't wait. Like I can't wait to start packing."

His smile turned to pure delight. "Taking Liam back to Melody's is going to hurt, but heading to Bali the next day definitely takes some of the sting out of it."

"Two weeks of wedded bliss."

His mouth dropped open comically. "I hope it's a lot more than two weeks!"

I laughed, tracing my hand down his thigh. "I'm sure of it. And when we get back, we have other things to look forward to. Like working on a brother or sister for Liam."

He placed his hand over mine, large and protective. "So many things to look forward to. But tonight is all about you and me. The rest can wait until tomorrow."

After dinner, we rose to applause and headed toward the Coral Queen. I hadn't been inside the lobby since my previous visit. The vacation that had started with a lonely woman nursing a broken heart and ended with a completely new life.

I nodded graciously as we swept past applauding people in the lobby. Quinn gripped my hand tighter, and I glanced up at him. His eyes held a slightly dazed look—mine had to be similar. I stared at the large Coral Queen etching behind the front desk, marveling that here I was again. Only now I was with Quinn, as it should have been all along.

Guess we've proven that you can go home again...

THANK you for reading *In Too Deep*! I hope you loved Steph and Quinn's story. This was such a fun book to write, and I loved how their second chance unfolded.

I'm happy to tell you Steph and Quinn make an appearance in the next Island Escapes book, *Beached in Bali*! So does Monica. If you enjoy a steamy, fun escape that immerses you in a different world, I think you'll enjoy it. Dawn and Cole are very near the top of the list of my favorite couples I've ever written about.

The island of Bali is an incredibly exotic, intoxicating place full of deep culture and exciting adventure.

Not to mention plenty of romance...

ABOUT BEACHED IN BALI:

**Best friends in Bali. A secret crush. One bed.
Could one week change our lives forever?**

Dawn:

I'm adrift in a sea of uncertainty, trying to figure out the woman in the mirror. All I ever wanted was a family, but my ex-husband blames me for its absence. After the divorce, I am embarking on an adventure to Bali, seeking who I'm supposed to be.

But I'm not alone. My best friend, Cole Foster, insists on joining me. He's so sweet I hardly notice how attractive and athletic he is. Really. We even booked separate rooms. Well, until a resort catastrophe forces us to share a bungalow.

And a bed.

Bali is supposed to clear my chaotic mind, but now my BFF is staring at me like I'm the answer to his wildest dreams. Can we leave our pasts behind and risk our friendship for a shot at love?

***Beached in Bali*, part of the Island Escapes series, is a sexy standalone romance set against an exotic tropical backdrop. It features an ugly duckling who doesn't believe he's a swan, and a woman torn between what's safe and what's worth risking.**

Check Out Beached in Bali!

I HOPE you enjoyed *In Too Deep*. If you'd like a glimpse into **Steph and Quinn's happily ever after**, click below to sign up for my newsletter:

Beach Read Update
(www.erinbrockus.com/ITD)

As a thank you, I'll send you a **bonus scene** which peeks into their lives several years in the future.

If you're already on my list, I've got you covered! At the bottom of each newsletter is a link to all my free content for subscribers. Just find your last email from me to read this bonus, as well as any others you might have missed. Or you can simply sign up again—you'll have your bonus in a flash.

Because of You: A Small Town Fake Relationship Romance

Memories of You: A Small Town Second Chance Romance

Shades of You: A Small Town Forbidden Romance

ASSOCIATED SHORT STORIES AND NOVELLAS:

Traces of You: A Small Town Rivals to Lovers Romance*

* Subscriber exclusive

HALF MOON BAY SERIES:

MAIN NOVELS:

Finding Hope: Half Moon Bay Book 1

Defending Hope: Half Moon Bay Book 2

Rising Hope: Half Moon Bay Book 3

Forever Hope: Half Moon Bay Book 4

Half Moon Whim: Half Moon Bay Book 5 (Standalone)

Half Moon Ember: Half Moon Bay Book 6 (Standalone)

Half Moon Aqua: Half Moon Bay Book 7

Crowning Hope: Half Moon Bay Book 8

Dive into steamy small-town romance, where passion meets paradise!

Award-winning author Erin Brockus writes steamy small town romances that transport readers to exotic, tropical destinations, and provide a perfect beachy getaway from everyday life. Her mature, relatable characters are impossible not to root for, and she weaves breezy romantic adventure into her stories, emphasizing scuba diving and the ocean.

Drawing on her twin passions for diving and travel, Erin infuses her characters and narratives with a sense of excitement and passion. Her idea of the perfect day involves sipping a cocktail on the beach after exploring the ocean depths.

Erin lives in Washington wine country with her husband, who is also a scuba instructor. She is currently hard at work on her next island adventure. When she's not writing, you might find her out for a run or cycling through the countryside on the next quest for adventure.